Simply To Die For

Maxine Douglas

Warning: Not intended for persons under the age of 18. May contain coarse language and mature content that may disturb some readers. Reader discretion advised.

Cover Art Design by: Kelly Moran/Rowan Prose Publishing
Photo Credit: Adobe Images
Editor: Katie O'Connor
First Printing
ISBN: 978-1-961967-42-7
Rowan Prose Publishing, LLC
www.RowanProsePublishing.com

Published in the United States of America

Praise for Maxine Douglas

"A root-worthy couple."
- InD'tale Magazine

"An intriguing story."
-Marsha Keeper Bookshelf

"A believable story that's enjoyable."
-Page by Page Inside Out Reviews

"The story unfolds beautifully."
-Essential Romance Book Club

"The characters were great, had chemistry, and the storyline was suspenseful."
-Book Wench

PROLOGUE

I turned and surveyed the room. It had been easier than I first imagined. None of them put up a fuss. Well, except the one I've left in a dark corner of the room, that is, and he's not a threat. Even his crying and whimpering have ceased. I only hope he'll live long enough to give them my message. If not, well, I'll think of another way to get her back and get that damn list of hers. Her royal highness, Kandi Kyses. What made her think she could quit the business and go into hiding? No one gets away with crossing me, as she'll soon discover. Did she think for one minute she wouldn't be found no

matter how far away she was? I have to give it to her though, these damn chocolates of hers are divine.

I placed the pink and white striped candy box in position carefully with my gloved fingers and chuckled.

Her handmade candies were... Simply to die for.

CHAPTER 1

Kandi Kisses Candies: Wisconsin

Clar smiled while stirring the chocolate, the contentment of being back home wrapping around her like a warm quilt. No sir, the glitter of LA was not for her. She loved moments like this when childhood memories of baking with her mother came to her. It felt as if mom was right there with her, laughing at the chocolate mustache the spinner would leave above her lip. Making chocolates was a way for Clar to stay connected to her.

Like taking those police science classes brought her closer to her dad. It had taken her so long after the accident to come alive again. And now becoming a professional candy maker firmed the link to her mom. She liked to think that her parents would be proud now.

A trifecta of disasters had sent her running—Dylan's death, Levi's subsequent freak-out, and her own personal sleazy newshound Jimmy O'Brien's constant harassment. It'd seemed like he was nipping at her heels; making her run with his constant questions about her career, her parents, specifically her dad, and Levi's reaction to Dylan's murder. Yes, as far as she was concerned Dylan Cameron had been murdered. But who was she? Just an empty-headed blonde adult film star.

She was glad to be out of those shark-infested waters of Hollywood, and nothing would ever induce her to return. Not even Levi's continued false cries for help.

Clar tried to push the past away, Dylan lying dead, of course people OD'ed every day but not friends, not like that. No wonder Levi had gone paranoid on her. She shivered; glad she'd taken the self-defense courses even though she didn't believe Levi's wild stories. It still made her feel safer, not that evil doers were likely to come knocking on her door in sleepy Lake Mills, Wisconsin. No, more like dozens of local children looking for Easter goodies.

With Easter just around the corner, she needed to make sure the chocolate bunnies were ready to be devoured by all the hungry boys and girls in town. Kandi Kisses was due to officially open the week before the scheduled Easter egg hunt in the downtown triangle. She'd been open on weekends only for the past six months. Her bank account finally acknowledged the ability to stay open six days a week and stop dipping into her savings.

She swiped a hand over a brow pushing bangs out of her eyes, then grabbed an ice-cold cola from the fridge, needing a break. One of her favorite cable shows, *LA Adult Entertainment Today*, kept her company in the background. *You watch it to see a glimpse of him,* Clar's inner critic snarked. Sadly, it was true. But listening to Jimmy's voice on occasion was not backing down.

Despite leaving LA a few years ago, she still felt the need to keep up on what was going on in Tinsel Town. Not that she wanted to go back to that life...ever, but Clar still had a few good friends there, not to mention people who needed her. Levi for instance called every couple of weeks with a new crisis. She smiled at the memory of her rescuer after her parents' deaths. Levi was an enigma, gay and working as a straight porn star.

Sometimes she thought he invented problems hoping to lure her back, not out of meanness, but because he missed her so much. It was touching really. She missed him too, but this nice quiet town was her life now and she wasn't leaving it. She felt safe and normal for the first time since leaving her hometown over twenty years ago. Lake Mills had changed, yet in many respects it hadn't. To her the small town feel of the place was comforting. Some of the people from her past had moved on to bigger and better things. Most didn't remember her from grade school and that was fine with Clar. She cherished the anonymity.

It made starting over a lot easier.

"An SXY exclusive." Everything in her tightened at his smooth voice. Damn, she'd been hoping to hear it, but it didn't stop her heart from quivering when it happened. She spun to look at the TV. Jimmy O'Brien! He looked as good and as snarky as ever as he smiled at the camera. She sucked in a breath sinking down on a chair. Why was she torturing herself this way, wanting someone she shouldn't? "Can a porn star actually go legit? That's the rumor out of Cum Again Studios. A sassy thirty-something sex kitten reported to have kicked the film business has opened a candy store, exact location unknown. Seductive, melt in your mouth, finger-lickin' good..."

She froze, every atom in her body on alert, and glared at the screen as he ratted her out on national TV. How could he stoop so low especially as he was the one who'd helped chase her out of town? The news report slammed through Clar as she sat still, barely breathing. She watched, appalled as one of her old "Kandi Kyses" headshots spattered across the screen with Cum Again Studios as a backdrop. At least they didn't use an old movie poster.

She hardly recognized the woman flashing before her. Long, flowing bleach blonde hair fell over a pair of manufactured Hollywood breasts barely covered in a T-shirt a couple of sizes too small. Thankfully, that woman no longer existed.

"I'm wondering if the candy is as tasteful as its namesake, former adult film star Kandi Kyses. I can't wait to see the molds she'll use for her chocolate. I somehow don't think this will be the old-fashioned corner candy store we grew up with.

For SXY, this is Jimmy O'Brien."

That son of bitch, how could he do this to her? All thoughts of candy making went out the window as soon as James O'Brien, reporter, and a royally attractive pain-in-her-ass, opened a door to her past she thought she'd bolted shut.

"Damn it, O'Brien! Why in the hell can't you leave me the hell alone?" Clar slouched against the green sofa pillows, worrying her bottom lip as anger crept through her. "Can't a woman start a new life without the press and its most persistent hound dog sniffing her out? You wanted me to run, I ran, so leave me the hell alone."

Grabbing her cell, Clar tapped in the number to the studio. Someone was fucking gonna pay for this breach of ethics. Damn it, her private info was supposed to remain just that, private. But she'd left enemies behind, Evie, the nasty receptionist for instance, kicking her off the set. Someone was obviously gunning for her. Well, they had another think coming if they thought she was just going to sit here and take it. Levi might know who'd leaked the story to the press. He was always up on studio gossip.

"You have reached Cum Again Studios," a recorded voice answered. "We are currently tied up and unable to take your call. Please leave a message and we will get back to you as soon as we are free. Thank you for calling Cum Again."

"Crap! Not now, I don't have time to play telephone tag," Clar growled at the mechanical voice as she paced the kitchen floor. After the beep, she said. "Please have Levi Andres call Clar Turner as soon as possible. Thank you."

Clar disconnected then checked the time. It was ten in the morning on the west coast, there should be someone at the studio by now manning the switchboard. Even if there was a shoot on location, someone would be in the office.

"We interrupt this program for breaking news!" Oh shit, what now? She poised herself for more bad news. Another reporter came on the screen looking very serious. At least it wasn't Jimmy this time.

"We interrupt this previously recorded program to bring you breaking news for SXY—this just in. Reports of an assault at Cum Again Studios earlier this morning are surfacing. Unconfirmed reports of at least six dead and one wounded. SXY has a reporter on the scene and will bring you up to date information as it becomes available. Stay tuned."

Oh shit, Levi! He was supposed to be shooting a new film there today. He'd laughed about it last week. Hands shaking, she punched in the studio's number again.

"Cum Again Studios," said a snide voice.

Clar breathed a sigh of relief in spite of the fact that it was Evelyn Dagmyer one of her least favorite people. "Evelyn, it's Kandi. What's going on? Is Levi..." She bit her lip unable to say the words she feared.

"Get off the phone, Kandi. You're not on the list of people I'm allowed to talk to," she said with a sniff.

As usual, the offensive woman's sharp tone held annoyance and disdain but there was something else that made Clar crumble inside. It sounded like she was holding back tears. What the hell? Evie didn't get emotional which meant. Oh hell.

"Let's skip our usual banter and get to the heart of the matter. Is Levi okay?"

"So now you care...interesting."

What the hell was that supposed to mean? It was Evie who'd fired her off the last set, inadvertently aiding in her departure. Now she was acting like Clar had abandoned them all.

"Tell me about Levi, damn you!"

"He's still..." her voice broke, making Clar's gut tighten.

"Let me," a low male voice said in the background.

"This is Detective Cameron, who am I speaking to?" The gruff male voice echoed with authority. A chill went through her at the officious voice with its Midwestern tone. Chicago maybe, she thought absently.

"This is Clar Turner. I'm trying to reach Levi Andres at Cum Again Studios. Is he...?" Clar's hand shook, feeling the pressure of tears behind her eyes. She could not afford to give into them, not now.

"Ah yes, Miss Turner," he said, adding, "I was just about to call you."

She closed her eyes and prayed softly. *Please let Levi be safe*.

"Yes," she said tensely as she heard a woman sobbing loudly in the background.

"Ms. Turner, yes, it's indicated you are Andres' only contact should something happen. Like I said, I was just getting ready to call you."

Oh gawd, this could not be happening. She felt like she was going to pass out. It was like Dylan all over again, but ten times worse. Levi loved life, he didn't do drugs, he was... She sniffed back tears. "Yes."

"Levi has been transported to a local hospital. He had been asking for you and the studio requests you return to LA as soon as possible."

She let out the breath she'd been holding, relief surging through her in a giddy wave. "He's alive. Why didn't you say that in the first place," she yelled, not caring that she was berating a cop. *Okay, calm down, you can't help Levi if you piss off the cops.* "Is he going to be okay? What happened?" She yanked an overnight bag from the top of the closet. She had to get to Levi.

"He's in surgery. The rest, Ms. Turner, the rest I'm afraid is a police matter, and cannot be discussed over the telephone."

"I'll be on the next flight." As soon as the words 'Levi' and 'surgery' were in the same sentence she'd mentally made plans to be by his side. Levi was hurt enough to go to the hospital, and she should have been there to protect him. She'd never believed his wild "they're out to get me" stories, and now he was hurt. Clar never should have left LA without him, or thought she could start over again.

"Check in with LAPD when you arrive. I need to talk to you before giving you clearance to see Mr. Andres."

So, she needed to go through this detective to get to Levi. Why? That didn't sound right but, in her haste, she didn't ask questions. "Yes, yes of course. Detective Cameron."

"Thank you for your cooperation, Ms. Turner, I'll be waiting for you." The emotionless voice confirmed, then faded away with the chatter behind it.

"Wait! Cameron?" Then the phone went dead. "Damn it!"

Clar threw some clothing in the overnight bag, grabbed several things, and headed out the door, punching the number of the one person she knew she could count on in a fight.

"I need you, Jackson. Can you meet me in LA as soon as possible? It's Levi this time."

Revolving Roses Ranch
Black Horse Canyon
Oklahoma

"That's a good boy. You'll feel better after we get this Oklahoma red dirt off you," Jackson Wolfe cooed as she ran the stiff bristled brush across the prized stud's back. Max, aka Black Ice, bobbed his head in agreement. He was such a sweet boy. The sleek Quarter Horse was the pride and joy of Revolving Roses Ranch and about the only decent thing that came of Jackson's grandfather's notorious Hollywood past and his singing cowboy royalties.

If not for Jacki's quick intervention, her father would have gambled the ranch away ten years ago in a high stakes poker game. That stunt of his cost Jacki most of her life savings, and forced her into eventually giving up a career as a private investigator. She'd been shoved into teaching through a school out of California to keep her and the ranch above water.

Max shifted slightly to the left, stretching his glistening ebony neck toward the pink and black striped box tilting precariously between the stall bars. Her latest guilty pleasure courtesy of her favorite self-defense student and BFF. "Oh no you don't, bad boy, those are mine!" Jacki grabbed the box an instant before Max's lips skimmed the shiny paper. "You know chocolate isn't good for you. Besides, Clar made these for me, not you." Jacki unwrapped one of the candies and popped it into her mouth.

Patting Max on the neck, Jacki smiled with satisfaction as the chocolaty flavor burst on her tongue and richness slid down her throat. Her BFF might be out of the movie business, but Clar was still setting off fireworks. These were orgasmic.

"Damn these are great. Clar's going to make a killing with them." Jacki ran her hand along the horse's back, down a sleek black leg, and pulled a hoof pick from her back pocket. Pinching just above the fetlock, she took the offered hoof in hand. She repeated the process three more times, removing the day's muck from around the frog of each hoof.

The clomping of boots raced towards Jacki as she gently released the last leg, standing upright to see who dared to run through the barn. The long-time foreman grabbed her arm and dragged her into the barn's office before she could muster up a complaint.

"Rusty, what the heck is going on. You know not to...."

Rusty Calhoon stood with the TV remote in his hand, gave her a worried look, and then turned to the adult cable channel 69. Jacki's stomach rolled when a photo of Kandi Kyses, Clar's semi-scandalous alias, appeared on the screen with Clar's tormentor James O'Brien giving commentary. *Oh hell, no.* What was it with those two? Why couldn't the man leave Clar alone? Clar had worked so hard to disappear. How could he out Clar like this? Because there was more going on than just their mutual antagonism. They'd always had a love/hate thing between them, but this was a gutter move on Jimmy's part, unless there was more behind it. He wasn't smiling, his jaw was tight, hell, even his body language was all wrong. It was as if someone was holding a gun to his head.

"...Kandi Kyses, whose sudden disappearance remained a mystery up until now. It's rumored that...Kandi Kisses...cherry poppin' guaranteed."

Distracted by her thoughts, Jacki leaned into the desk, barely listening to Jimmy give his report. The man nearly drove her best friend, Clar Turner, insane before she left the industry. Truth be told, between Jimmy constantly reporting her every move and Levi's continuous drama, and Dylan's tragic overdose, any sensible woman would have gone off the deep end. She respected Clar for breaking free and making her own life.

A few moments passed and another reporter came on. "Breaking news for SXY—this just in. Reports of an assault at adult filming studio,

Cum Again Studios, ... Numerous dead and wounded have been reported... Stay tuned."

Jacki's jaw dropped. This could not be happening. The phone rang in the barn and the answering machine kicked in. Clar's garbled voice, scared and panicky, echoed in the barn. "I need you...LA...Levi." Jacki turned down the volume, walked out of the office, untied Max and put him in a stall.

"Rusty, call the airport. I want the ranch plane ready within the hour with the shortest flight path to LAX."

Ocean Beach
Los Angeles, California

Maybe it was the way the tip had come in wrapped in a pink and black striped box. Or, maybe it was the way someone seemed to be setting Clar up. Either way, things didn't add up to James O'Brien's liking. It sucked that he'd been forced to out her but at least he'd held back her location. The station manager would probably have his ass for that but he didn't care. He had walked through the newsroom watching each foot fall on the cold gray tile floor, cursing. The waves called and he was all too happy to finally answer their allure and lose himself in the oblivion. It had been weeks since he waxed up his board and right now, he badly needed to clear his head.

Damn, she was really gonna hate him now, and this time for good reason. This time he wasn't trying to do her a favor and save her ass by running her out of town. He'd fought for months to get the news report on Kandi Kyses squelched. And then fate in the form of a black and pink striped candy box had forced his hand. Whoever was doing the hack job on Kandi had simply bypassed him to send the proof to his boss, and he'd had no choice but to break the story. It was either that or let one of the other less merciful reporters do it. No fucking way that was happening.

His past investigative training told him it was a set up, but who was behind it, and why? The overdose death of Dylan Cameron, Levi, one of his sources and Kandi's best friend plunged into paranoia, and then the planned mysterious and sudden retirement of Kandi Kyses. There was a pattern here but why couldn't he put two and two together?

To the average Joe, this would be an isolated incident. To Jimmy, the dots connected a common thread...something weird was happening at Cum Again Studios. Maybe a day of riding the surf would clear his mind...a guy could hope, couldn't he?

The waves were great, taking Jimmy's mind off Clar for moments at a time. The sport he'd grown to love usually relaxed him, freeing up his soul. Not today. The freedom of riding his board did little to ease his troubled mind.

Wiping down his board, he bade farewell to his surfing buddies. Climbing into his black Durango, he grabbed his cell phone checking for messages...six from the station in rapid fire. What the hell, had World War III started, or maybe another celebrity sex tape had surfaced. He punched in his code.

"Damn it, O'Brien! Where the hell have you been? Get your worthless ass over to CAS and call me on the way. There's a fucking bloodbath over there." His boss's words, laced with arsenic and urgency, boomed into his ear. "I'll have a team on standby, so unless you're dead too you'd better heed my call!"

Unless I'm dead too? Oh fuck! Checking the time stamp of the message, Jimmy noted that call came in right after he'd hightailed it out of the station and turned off his phone. Shit, how could the world have come apart in the interim? Scrolling through the remaining missed calls, he noted the first one had come in more than four hours ago. Had he really been on the beach for so long?

Shoving the key into the ignition, he slipped the SUV into gear and instructed his phone panel to call the station. Adrenaline pounded in his ears. The ring of the phone sounded like sonar from a submarine, as he toweled himself dry.

"Where the hell are you?"

"Just got off the beach." Jimmy tossed the towel into the back. "What's going on? What's the mess at CAS this time?"

The silence was black as the deep recesses of a cave. Jimmy's heart skipped a beat and the hairs on the back of his neck prickled.

"Bodies everywhere. Levi Andres is one of them."

CHAPTER 2

Jimmy's gut tensed when he saw the crime scene tape roping off CAS. A young cop stood guard at the door. Cripe, the kid still had acne and looked like he'd just joined the force, nervous as all hell. The first thing you learned in his business was the art of getting around greenhorn cops. He smiled to disarm the kid, waved his press credentials under the kid's nose, and ducked under the tape.

The cop hanging around the door stared at the press pass being waved under his broken one too many times nose. "Hold it right there," the cop said, his voice cracking.

"James O'Brien, SXY." Jimmy flipped open his notebook, breathing steadily to calm his pounding heart. His connection to Clar couldn't be exposed if at all possible. "What can you tell me about the attack?"

"You'll have to talk to the officer in charge."

"O'Brien, what the hell are you doing in my crime scene?" The annoyingly familiar gruff Midwest accent grated on Jimmy's nerves. Talk about a blast from the past. More like a grenade that'd blown his life apart before. *His crime scene! What the fuck?* He turned to see Reed Cameron rocking back on his heels looking as ominous as he'd last seen him that fateful Chicago night seven years ago. He was older and heavier but the same gruff SOB nonetheless. *Crooked cop, in the pocket of the DeLuca family, ran me out of Chicago years ago. So, what is he doing here? The DeLuca's turf doesn't extend this far.* Then he saw the black and pink striped candy box with Kandi Kisses written on it in Cameron's beefy hand and froze. It was stained with blood and sealed in an evidence bag. His gut turned to ice. What the hell was going on?

"A bit out of your jurisdiction, isn't it, Cameron?" Much as he wanted to take a swing at the man, he held back. He needed to find out what was going on pronto...before it got to Clar...although looking at the candy box it seemed that was a moot point. This couldn't be good. A dirty Chicago cop with known mob ties at a murder scene at a west coast porn studio? When in the hell had he come to California, and for what? If he connected him to Clar, things could go from bad to worse to impossible far too quickly. Jimmy flipped to a clean page and wrote *SOB. Chicago.*

"None of your damned business, you washed up scum bag reporter. So don't fuck with me or my people. I got rid of you in Chicago and I can do it here." Cameron spat out with venom.

That night was seared into Jimmy's memory. He had been following up some leads from an informant and decided to make an unannounced visit to the Chicago mayor's office after hours one night. Detective Reed Cameron arrived just after Jimmy broke in and found the documents he needed to throw the mayor out of office.

Cameron burst in gun drawn with a platoon of plain clothes men in tow, many looking more like hired guns than officers of the law. Jimmy had gotten off light thanks to Cameron, so he guessed he should have thanked him back then. He'd only lost his job, and his credibility, not his life. Jimmy had been forced into an early retirement after a trumped-up newspaper article. He was advised to keep his mouth shut or suffer the consequences. He didn't fancy having his mug on a missing person's poster or being fitted for a pair of cement boots. Shutting up, which for him was hard to do, and disappearing had seemed the only option. And he'd gone to LA and reinvented himself as a tabloid reporter after nearly draining his bank account living on the beach. It was miles away from the hard-hitting journalism he'd once practiced and while he didn't cover the latest gang drive-by or the current elections, it paid the rent.

Clearing the distance between them in three steps, Cameron's rigid posture attempting to throw authority around something Jimmy no longer feared. The fact that Cameron was in LA spoke volumes; there's been a falling out of some sort or another, but what? Last Jimmy knew, Cameron had been tight with the DeLuca family. So why was he here? What, if anything, had severed that relationship?

"I hope you're not here as a reporter." Cameron took a step closer, his husky body ramrod straight. Jimmy could smell stale gyros on his breath as he hissed. "You remember the agreement, don't you? And the consequences?"

"And I hope that you're not here as a crooked cop. The DeLuca's have no power here." He saw Cameron wince at the mention of his mob bosses and wondered about it. "You can't hurt me here, Detective." Jimmy smiled, tapping his notebook. "I'm wondering why it is you happen to be in sunny California and at the scene of a murder no less."

"Humph, shows how good your skills are these days, O'Brien. If you'd been on the side of the cops, you'd have known I came on board a few months ago." Cameron stood inches from Jimmy. A dark sadness flashed in Cameron's eyes, then he jabbed a finger into Jimmy's chest. "Stay. Out. Of. My. Way."

Jimmy swiped the warning away, then came nose to nose with his former adversary. "Is that a threat, Detective?"

"Take it any way you like, O'Brien." Cameron turned then stomped past the LA officers and detectives going through papers and reviewing a statement from the receptionist, Evelyn Dagmyer. Jimmy knew he'd gotten to Cameron; he'd seen red creep up that grimy neck of his.

Jimmy might have won this encounter. He wasn't about to let his guard down for a moment—not this time. He turned and spotted the officer who'd been at the door when he'd arrived. He might be able to worm some information out of the rookie.

Years back, Clar's father had been one of the cops who turned in several of the mob's insiders. Karl Turner was dedicated to the ideals of law enforcement and built his life around it. While Clar was tucked away at UCLA, he'd been about to retire after thirty years of service. Karl and his wife Candyss were California bound to join her when they were killed. Jimmy believed that somewhere deep inside, Cameron knew Clar's parents' accident was anything but, which made his appearance here all the more alarming. He wove his way through the policemen, and tapped the officer on the shoulder hoping this time he'd caught him a bit distracted.

"So, tell me officer, is Levi Andres dead and where did you get the candy box?"

⸺ ✑ ⸺

Clar slung her bag over a shoulder and wove through the crowd. LAX swarmed with people and she needed to find a taxi before the droves of other people did. She glanced at a wall clock then stepped through the doors to snag a ride to LAPD when a sharp whistle caught her attention.

Shading her eyes from the morning sun, she caught a glimpse of a cowboy hat. Clar leaned slightly to the right and smiled. Under a cream-colored Stetson was a shock of auburn waves and a face she'd hoped to see...Jackson Wolfe.

"Thanks for coming, and it's good to see you." Clar hugged her friend and burst into tears.

"Let's go, Jacki," she sniffed, "I need to find out what happened."

"You know me, I had to be here for my BFF. While my plane was being readied, I did some digging on my own, but the cops won't tell me anything. Even with my contacts lingering around the precinct, I hit a dead end. No one is talking, so either they haven't much to go on or they've been told to keep a lid on it." Jacki pulled the black F-150 rental onto I90 and headed toward the 110 to downtown LA and police headquarters. "Evidently Jimmy O'Brien was one of the reporters at the scene so I'm betting he'll show up sooner than later."

Clar sighed and settled her head against the headrest. Jimmy was the last person she wanted to see. "Maybe you can help me avoid him, Jacki. I'm not up to him or his school-boy-crush antics."

"Tell me what you know, Clar, and maybe I can help figure this out. I've checked the medical examiner's office, and my old contact there told me Levi Andres wasn't brought in to their facility, or any other for that matter. Which tells me he's alive somewhere, probably in protective custody at a local hospital. If that's so, you'll have to go to the station, find out where they have him, and get clearance to see him. Barging in at every hospital in LA will only land us in jail and unable to do any good. When was the last time you talked to Levi?"

"I don't remember exactly. It's been a couple of weeks or so. Everything seemed fine. He sounded the happiest I've heard him in years. I felt like he'd finally come to terms with Dylan's death." She sighed, chewing on her bottom lip. She tried to focus on the passing buildings as her world fell apart around her. "Yesterday I was making bunnies, thinking of my parents, and today..."

"Bunnies?"

"Molds for Easter. Grand opening was supposed to be this weekend." Clar sucked back the urge to cry. Everything she worked for was about to go down the drain. Her life nothing but a heap of dirty laundry she'd tried to desperately get to the cleaners. Mentally shaking the thoughts away, she took a deep breath and steadied herself for whatever happened next. "Anyway, LA Adult Entertainment Today came on as usual and I didn't pay too close attention until I heard Jimmy say how 'Kandi Kysses' had retired to make chocolates. I was so flabbergasted, I immediately picked up the phone to call Levi."

"And he wasn't there," Jacki said gently.

"Right." Tears stung Clar's eyes. The what ifs had been plaguing her since she'd heard the news. What if she'd never left Levi, what if she believed all his sky is falling calls for help. She sighed.

"When did you talk to the police?"

"Just before I called you. Before that I called the studio right after I heard O'Brien's report to ask Levi if he knew who'd leaked my information. I got no answer, so I had to leave a message. I called back a second time after the news of the assault, this time Evie Dagmyer answered with her usual bitchiness saying they were busy, only to have the phone taken from her." Clar closed her eyes, trying to chase away the reminders of the sorrowful sobbing she'd heard during that call and shuddered. Evelyn was always so tightly controlled. To have her go off the deep end that way. It was shocking. Something about Evelyn Dagmyer always set off her warning bells, no more so than yesterday. "That's when the police told me about Levi. Also, it sounded like a woman, at least I think it was a woman, crying in the background. Lots of muffled voices and the cop would only tell me that I was to come to LA and report to Detective Cameron immediately upon my arrival."

"Cameron, wasn't that Dylan's last name?" Jacki stepped on the gas and jockeyed for position on the 110.

"Yes, and that's when the investigative training you gave me kicked in and I called you.

Something tells me this is more than a coincidence."

CHAPTER 3

LAPD

"Come on, Sergeant! There's been a murder and you've got to give me something to report." Jimmy hounded the disheveled man behind the chipped and stained counter, hoping he'd push him enough that he would spill something newsworthy. Most of all he needed ammunition against Cameron. The guy always had an angle, and it was never on the side of the angels. Was

Cameron colluding on the frame up job someone was doing on Clar?

Jimmy needed something, anything, to give Clar when he talked to her. She may not appreciate his report on her, and she may very well verbally send him into the middle of next week, regardless, he wanted to ease her fears about Levi. "Basically, a massacre at a film studio and you guys are as tight lipped as a virgin at an orgy. People want to know what the hell happened, damn it!"

"There's nothing that hasn't already been said. Now if you'll find your way out, I've got things to do." The officer turned his back and stepped over to his desk, shuffling papers around, trying to look like he had something more important to do.

"Damn it! What the hell happened over there?" Jimmy stood his ground, unrelenting. They didn't call him a pain in the ass newshound for nothing. He needed to know if Levi was dead or alive. Someone needed to tell Clar before she heard it on the news—and that someone should be him.

"I thought I made it perfectly clear you were to butt out and stay clear of this. Anymore lip out of you and you'll be cooling your heels in a cell."

"O'Brien—what the hell do you want?" Cameron slithered out of his office toward him, venom glistening in his cold eyes. So, the oily bastard was here all the time, he must have been laughing his ass off listening to Jimmy try to get something out of the cop.

"Sir," the young cop said.

Cameron turned to look at a young officer nervously standing a few feet from him. "What?" he spat as if the man were nothing more than a spittoon.

"She's here." The officer lowered his voice, glancing toward the elevators.

Jimmy went stiff as a board and looked toward the elevator too. Everything that had been building in him seemed to go on point. The doors swooshed open and a redhead in jeans, shirt, and cowboy hat stepped out, and Jimmy let out the breath he'd been holding. No Clar, maybe she wasn't coming. Even though he knew she was safer away from the scene, he was disappointed. Nevertheless, there was something about the redhead that caught his attention, especially when she turned to glare in his direction. Jimmy thought he caught the smell of horses and a "there's a new sheriff in town" attitude as her scornful glare raked over him before stopping and deepening on Cameron. Okay, it seemed Clar had brought a posse of one and thank God for that.

The woman surveyed the area before moving aside for a full-figured, casually dressed thirty-something woman with dark spiked hair who stepped off the elevator with fire in her eyes and purpose in her step.

Clar!

He thought he'd been prepared, he wasn't. His heart twisted, his senses sharpening, even after all this time. Their gazes locked as if she was a heat seeking missile and he her target. Jimmy's heart raced as he shifted to ease the sudden pressure in his jeans. He'd know her anywhere, no matter how much she changed her appearance. Some things could never change, her essence, her spirit. She smiled just enough for him to become uncomfortable and he wondered what she was thinking about him. That he was a jerk for outing her on his program undoubtedly. How did she find out about the killings? Same as everyone else, stupid, through the news. However, she doesn't know about the candy box. Oh shit, he had to warn her about the set up. "We need to talk, honey."

"Don't you dare honey me," she scowled at him.

"Beat it, O'Brien, unless you want me to toss your useless ass in jail." Cameron stepped in his way. "Can't you see the lady doesn't want you here?"

Cameron held out his hand. "Ms. Turner, thank you for coming so quickly. I'm sorry to have you fly half-way across the country like this. Please, step into my office, we've got a few questions regarding Levi Andres, and other things."

"Where's Levi?" Clar turned her gaze from Jimmy, and the electricity between them fizzled out. The sense of falling under a wave, drowning under the curl as it pounded, hit Jimmy. The woman was sexier now than she'd ever been on the screen. Healthier was the word floating through his mind. Natural woman. She still held power over him, a power he'd love nothing more than to harness one of these days. If ever they could stop sniping at each other. He was ready for a wild and crazy ride. Maybe when this was all over...

"Ms. Turner, please, let's talk in my office." The detective took Clar by the elbow, guiding her into his glass-encased office. Cameron looked at Jimmy through slitted eyes, then turned an unnatural smile on Clar. "It's much more pleasant and you'll be able to tell me what you know without any outside interference."

Clar yanked her arm from Cameron's grip. The untidy man's intensity sent a shiver of warning through her. What had Jimmy been trying to warn her about? She looked back through the door to see Jimmy and Jacki talking. Jacki's eyes were wide and she shot a glare at Cameron through the door. *Oh shit.* This couldn't be good. Jacki had good instincts where bad guys were concerned. Yet it wasn't Jimmy she was suspicious of by the expression on her face, it was the detective. Clar turned to focus on Cameron. What was he trying to pull? She didn't like the hostile vibes coming off him from his wrinkled suit to the way he furrowed his eyes as if he were accusing her of doing something wrong. She didn't want to talk to him. Didn't want to be in this glass box he called an office with him. She needed to get to Levi.

Cameron pushed the door closed and turned to glower at her.

Clar watched him trying to figure out what he wanted. In the movies, this was where the evil theme music would come in, unfortunately, this was scary, real-life drama and she didn't have the time for his theatrics.

Jacki shoved her way into the room, the door bumping against his back, making him grunt and move out of the way. "Sorry, but she's not doing this alone." The low Texas growl held a threat even Clar would heed.

She smiled. Jacki wasn't the type of woman who would hesitate to tangle with Cameron, she'd put him flat on his back if necessary.

Wrestling steers most of your life will do that to you...man or woman. She'd chased down the best of them in the LA criminal underbelly. One overzealous cop, with an obvious hidden agenda, wouldn't deter her.

"Too bad, because it's her I want to talk to, not a pretty cowgirl with horse shit on her boots." Cameron pushed the door into Jacki and held it in position. "Now get the fuck out of here before I..."

"Here's the deal, Detective, about that 'pretty little cowgirl'. You let Jackson Wolfe stay in here or I walk." Clar waited, enjoying the greasy detective squirm in his under-starched, high-waisted pants. She took a step toward the door where Jacki had a boot-clad foot jammed into it. "It's totally up to you."

Clar waited and began to count. *One, two, three, four...what a sleaze bag...five, six, seven...does he have a connection to Dylan...eight, nine, ten...son-of-a-bitch!* She smiled, batted her eyes, and then looked Cameron square in the face. "This has been your decision, not mine. There's someone lying in a hospital bed that needs me, obviously you've decided you don't, seeing that you're into playing games. So, unless you are going to arrest me and throw me in jail, I'm leaving."

"That's a thought, Ms. Turner." Cameron held the door fast against the boot wedged in it.

"I think I could arrange it if you insist. Maybe you'd like to share a cell with your boyfriend out there." His sick grin turned her stomach. "Where were you between six and nine a.m.?"

She stared at him in shock. Was he accusing her of hurting Levi and the others? "At home making chocolates," she said.

"Like these," he said, pulling an evidence bag out of a shelf and putting it on his desk along with blood spattered candy wrappers.

She gulped looking down at her signature black and pink striped candy box, the handwritten candy wrappers done by yours truly. *Impossible* her mind screamed seeing the blood spatter on them. Gagging, she turned away sure she was going to barf all over the sleazebag. But then he had it coming.

Through the window she saw Jimmy take one look at her no doubt bloodless face, swear, and push off from the wall. He looked at the candy box a grim recognition in his eyes. He knew about this, had been trying to warn her, that is why Cameron had threatened him with jail. She shook her head and Jimmy stilled, although the glare on his face said he didn't like it. She sucked in a deep breath and turned to face Cameron who was standing there gloating like a shark about to strike. More like a bottom feeding barracuda. "Where did you get that box?"

He smirked. "Where do you think?"

It was the smirk that got to her the most. That he could be chortling while people, her former coworkers, and friends, lay dead and injured made her want to punch him. "So, you didn't send your old pals and fuck buddies some chocolates?"

She glared at him, treating the nasty question with disdain as it deserved. No way was she going to lower herself to his level. Bullies were really cowards on the inside. It was high time she went on the offensive. "No, but I need to know who did. Do you think you can figure that out or do I need to hire an outside PI and forensic technician?" Clearly, he hadn't been expecting that response because he rocked back on his heels.

"You keep thinking, Detective, because as of now I'm taking this out of your jurisdiction." She turned to Jacki, "You got all that?"

"Damn straight," Jacki said, thumping the door against his side once more. "I'll call in Lee from forensics, and put my best people on the case. Plus, I got that information you wanted."

Clar nodded, heading toward the door. Jacki bumped it against Cameron again and Clar slipped past him.

"Now wait just a minute," Cameron bellowed.

"Like I said, arrest me or I'm gone. When you feel like actually cooperating and solving this case, I'm sure you can figure out where to find me." She walked away on that exit line, proud that she didn't give in to her urge to kick him. Now she just had to rescue Levi, solve a murder, figure out who was out to get her, and work with Jimmy O'Brien. He looked just as wonderful as the day she told him to get the hell away from her and stay away. Damn, one of these days ...

CHAPTER 4

"So, you can do all those things you said you could, right?" Clar asked as Jacki weaved her way into the Los Angeles traffic, Clar riding shotgun, Jimmy in the back where they could both keep an eye on him.

"Piece of cake," Jacki said, undeterred by Clar's snort. "I called in a few favors. Simon Lee is coming out of retirement to do the forensics, and you've got the best in the business examining Cameron's every move."

"Like I can afford that," Clar said with a long, low sigh, the stress catching up with her.

"What stuff?" Jimmy asked from the back seat.

It was kind of a novel experience that there was something she knew the newshound didn't. She and Jacki shared a look before she turned to him. "Thanks for trying to warn me about the evidence against me."

"Ah, so he hit you with the candy box, the wrappers."

"Pretty much," she said, her stomach roiling when she remembered the blood.

"Deep breaths in and out," Jimmy coached, leaning forward to touch her shoulder. "It was in his hand when I showed up at CAS. Already tagged and bagged. Given my history with him, it was probably planted."

"Why don't I like the doubtful way you say probably," she asked seeing the worry in his eyes.

"Because you can read me way too well for my liking and you're smart."

She watched him bite his lip knowing he hated revealing that much about what made him tick. The truth behind the sleazy newshound.

"And also, because one of them showed up at my studio, sans blood, of course."

She saw the sincerity, heard the grit in his voice. Of course, it was why he'd sounded grumpy when he outed her on national TV.

"Whoever did this sent you a box of chocolates?"

He nodded. "And when that didn't work, they sent one to my boss."

So at least that mystery of how I was located is solved. "Thank you."

"For what, outing you?"

"No, for trying to protect me."

"Yeah, I'm some hero." He shook his head. "At least I can give you some information. Levi's at St. Vincent's over on West Third, in ICU in an induced coma. They've got a guard on him. At least that's what my source says."

She watched Jimmy check his seatbelt, making sure it was good and tight. The way Jacki was driving, she'd hoped they'd get there in one piece.

"Hey, you know how to get to the hospital, cowboy?"

"Where do you think we're heading, newshound," Jacki snorted.

Clar chuckled before turning her head. "Jacki's got sources you never even dreamed of."

"Great, so you don't need me for this either," he said under his breath.

She was surprised that he looked so unhappy. "Stick around, O'Brien, I just might need you yet." She smiled when that got a startled response. "Relax, she used to be a private detective plus she knows these streets better than most and it's not 'cowboy'. James O'Brien, meet Jackson Wolfe, and find a way to get along with her. Jacki and I go way back."

"Jackson Wolfe, as in the late and great singing—"

Jacki glared at him in the rearview mirror. Guess he hit a nerve. Either there was no love lost in the family or she didn't want to discuss her crooning relative. Most likely both if the old time Hollywood movie cowboy were true to form. The Jackson Wolfe he'd heard about was notorious around Tinseltown, and at one time had a big ranch somewhere in Texas. Or was it Oklahoma?

"Yes, as in. What can you tell us, O'Brien? I won't have her caught off guard again. Not on my watch."

Jimmy drew in a breath, gazing out the window. How in the hell was he going to tell her about Levi. Far as he figured, they were still like brother and sister. Then there was the thug trying to frame her or rattle her cage or both. Clar wouldn't want it all prettified for her sake; she'd want the truth and nothing more. He'd try to spare her as much as possible, even if there were no guarantees to the pain it may cause.

"Shit, Clar, are you really sure you want to hear this? It's not very pretty and the facts are murky at best." He studied her looking for any indication he should hold back. "The cops are keeping a tight lid on things for some reason. Wouldn't even let me in the crime scene. Cameron greeted me at the gate, candy box in his hand already tagged, bagged, and bloody. Seemed like he didn't know about our connection."

"He does now," she said, matter of factly.

"Like I said, so far, I've officially got squat. Nothing is written in stone yet; you know how an investigation runs. Reporters are always the last totem on the pole to get the straight facts."

"Yeah, like I'm going to believe that. You've always had your finger on the pulse of this city and from what I see nothing's changed. Just tell me. I don't want any surprises when I walk into that hospital room."

Now there's the Clar I know and love! Strong, loyal as hell to her friends, and this was going to tear her up.

"Fine, here are the facts as I know them. Everyone on the set was killed, every soul except Levi. Although I think he was left for dead given the amount of blood at the scene. He's in pretty rough shape." Jimmy flipped through his notes, wasting as much time as possible. She'd want to know about the candy box. He didn't want to tell her that it had been propped on Levi's body, deliberately soaked in his blood. Her wrappers strewn around the crime scene like obscene confetti. "Levi's hurt bad, honey.

Bruised ribs are the least of his problems, facial fractures, possible brain damage, like I said the doctors are keeping him in an induced coma. There may be permanent damage. It's too soon to tell.

"There's more." He took a deep breath and flipped his notebook closed. "You saw the candy box and wrappers that were scattered throughout the set. It's clear that someone is setting you up"

"I got news for you, Jimmy. I kind of figured that out when Cameron cornered me," Clar said. "If they want a war, they'll get one."

"It's either a message or someone's trying to set you up, Clar." Jacki pulled into the hospital lot and parked the truck. "This could be far more involved than we thought. Especially if O'Brien is telling the truth about them also sending the candy to his studio."

"I am," he said, looking her straight in the eye.

"How'd it come, Snail Mail, Fed Ex, UPS?" Jacki asked.

"I'm not sure. The mail delivery service dropped it in my slush pile one day. When I opened it, I thought she was..." Jimmy's voice trailed off.

"Sending you sweets," Jacki said.

"I'm sorry, I didn't think...?" Clar said.

"I'd wanna get 'em," he finished. "Anyhow, when I saw the note that came with 'em I tossed them in the trash."

"Shit, so I can't get prints off it," Jacki said sourly.

"My boss still has his. He's been hoarding the damned things; greedy bastard won't share. The jerk even special ordered two more boxes."

"Oh, so that's the special order that came to my online shop," Clar said. "I wondered when it came in seeing that my online business hasn't officially launched yet."

"I think someone is out to hurt you."

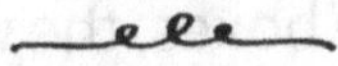

"Given the evidence I'd be a fool not to agree, but that isn't important now. I need to get to Levi." Clar jumped out of the car and started walking, blinking away the tears of rage and fear threatening to spill. Levi may or may not be Levi any more. Who would beat a guy as harmless as Levi just to send her a message?

"Easy," Jimmy said coming up beside her, taking her arm when she almost smacked into a parked car.

"Geez, Jimmy!" Clar exclaimed, trying to pry his fingers from her arm. "Thanks, but can you release your iron clad grip?"

Jacki trotted up beside her, flicking on the recorder she used for notes. Clar remembered it well from her old PI days. So, Jacki was on the job. Go team. Not that they stood much of a chance against Cameron.

"You haven't officially sold your candies on-line yet?" Jimmy asked.

"That's right, I sent out samples to a few friends."

"Like me," Jacki said with a smile.

"Right. Other than that, my buyers have been local. People showing up at my door, a few at the local gift shop that stocks some of my things."

"What about the boxes, the wrappers?" Jimmy asked. "Where do you get them?"

Clar shrugged. "I buy my wrappers online, the boxes too. I'm sure many others do the same thing as it's a popular outlet in the industry. Kandi Kisses wrappers are pink with black stripes on them when they arrive. I can spend hours at night watching TV hand stamping each one of the with the store name on them."

"They were solid pink in the beginning with the store's name scrolled across them, remember?" Jacki pointed out.

Clar sucked in a breath, holding it for a moment, trying to recall the exact color of the wrappers Cameron had shoved in her face. Oh my God, even bloodstained as they were, she could swear they were pink. "Yes, I changed them after the supply of the current ones ran out. I used to handwrite Kandi Kisses on them.

"This is crazy. No one in California should have access to my old candy wrappers." She saw Jacki and Jimmy share a troubled look and realized the situation was severe. Levi's attackers were trying to rattle her, to scare her, and damn, it was working. *Think. Why Cameron's animosity? And what about the pain in his eyes? And what was with him and Jimmy?*

She'd only been open on weekends a few months now for the early tourists and special events. Kandi Kisses wasn't scheduled to open full-time until this weekend. Now even that was on hold, if it ever happened after this. Once she got back, she'd have to check her books, but not once did she remember shipping candy to anyone but Jacki. Oklahoma wasn't California by any means. Her blood boiled to think someone would go to this extreme just to get her attention. She drew in a deep breath, her body relaxing for a few moments.

"Jimmy, what do you know about Detective Cameron? The one who looks like Jimmy Hoffa."

"Dirty cop. Formerly from Chicago PD. In the pocket of the DeLuca family."

"Like hell," Jacki said. "LAPD has some standards. They wouldn't have hired him if that were true, and…"

Jimmy snorted. "Yeah well, give it to me chapter and verse. We both know that's a load of bull or you'd probably still be working there."

"Chicago," Clar said thinking for a moment. "Do you think he knew my dad?"

"Yes," Jimmy said softly. "They were in the same precinct for twenty years."

She shivered, then held her breath. Her father was known to turn in dirty cops. If Cameron was as dirty as Jimmy said this animosity could go way back. She'd always had a suspicion what happened to her parents was no accident. "Was he on my dad's list of dirty cops?"

"That I don't know. But Cameron is connected to the DeLuca family, or at least he was at one time. There may have been a falling out and that's why he's here."

Old sins could cast long shadows. Hell, she'd never believed the convenient story of her parents' deaths. Now coming on the heels of Levi's attack it was too much. Her knees were going to buckle and only Jimmy and Jacki's support was keeping her upright. She needed to rescue Levi, solve the crime, and find out the truth about her parents. But first, she had to know what she was up against. "Is there anything more we need to know about Cameron and his mob connection?"

Jimmy shifted slightly, running his hands through sun-kissed hair. Clar itched to smooth the worried look from his face. Her fingers tin-gled from want to massage the tension from his neck. There was a history between Jimmy and Cameron, she needed to know what it was. "Tell me why you don't trust him."

"A long and old story, but let's cut to the chase by saying he's a scumbag detective from Chica-go who thought he was the next godfather to be. We had a run in while I was on my beat in Chicago; he ran me out of town and away from investigative journalism. I didn't like the idea of wearing cement overshoes, so here I am. What he's doing here, now, I couldn't tell you. Covering red carpet events as I do now, he and I have never crossed paths."

"Shit," Jacki turned, looking at them both.

"Precisely," Jimmy cut in, "And now here he is fitting us both for a jail cell."

Clar found out what room Levi was in af-ter proving she was indeed Clarice Turner with every piece of ID she could produce. The nurse, bless her heart, didn't want to let them all up to ICU but Clar convinced her that Jacki and Jimmy were medical experts specializing in emotional trauma. A few tears and sniffles and they were on their way.

They stepped off the elevator passing room after room until finally, at the end of the hall, was Levi's unmanned room. A surge of fear slammed through Clar.

"Where the hell are the cops?" Clar questioned loudly as they walked up to Levi's room in the ICU wing. "He's supposed to have a guard."

"Damn Cameron and his uncooperative hide," Jacki hissed.

"We've got this," Jimmy said, standing by Clar's side.

"I'll take care of it," Jacki promised, punching in numbers on her cell while heading back down the hall.

"Bless her. She's got more contacts than the LAPD and FBI combined."

Jimmy touched her arm. He must have sensed she was stalling, bracing herself. She allowed herself the luxury of leaning against him for a moment, absorbing his strength. So, Cameron was responsible for wrecking his life, changing his path. It gave her a new insight into him.

Clar pushed the door open. There were no words to describe the shell of the person she loved as a brother. At first, she couldn't even absorb the ghastly impact on her psyche. Levi had tubes coming out of his mouth, an IV in one hand, and his face was bandaged except for his eyes and mouth. She couldn't imagine what waited under the sterile white blanket and sheet. He looked so small lying there, so helpless, rage thrust through her pain.

Rage ignited through her like a wildfire burning every part of her being. She would make whoever did this very sorry.

"I'm sorry, no one is allowed in this room." A nurse continued checking fluids and writing something down, not giving them the simple courtesy of a glance.

Clar's gaze moved over Levi to the starchily dressed nurse standing next to the bed. Clar drew in the anger churning in her stomach. She hated being ignored as if she didn't exist, but realized it was misdirected. She wasn't really angry at the nurse. Still, Levi needed an advocate and she'd be his voice. "I understand about hospital rules, nurse. What I don't understand is why he's lying there unprotected. Where is his guard? I was told he had a twenty-four-hour guard. So where is he?"

"LAPD, you'll all have to leave, now!" She sucked in a breath. The command came from behind them with an authority that held a blend of menace and Texas charm. Okay, so he did have a guard, a sneaky one.

She turned, her gaze meeting green eyes that held serious intent to the extreme with a strong jaw line that matched. There was nothing middle-of-the-road about the man, and the sight of him immediately put up her guard. Every inch from his expression to his wide stance and scuffed cowboy boots screamed serious as hell.

Jimmy's surprised smile lit up his face and Clar remembered why she lusted after him in the first place. He was drop-dead-irresistible when he smiled. His smile sparkled in his brown eyes with a warmth and brightness that welcomed anyone inside. But when had he become friendly with the cops? And why this cop in particular? He'd always avoided them whenever possible like they were public enemy number one.

"Clint?"

"Jimmy, how the hell are you?" Clint's chiseled features softened for a moment, revealing what Clar's granny would have labeled as 'good old cowboy' material.

"You know each other?" Clar stood between the two, annoyed once again at being ignored.

"Clar, this is an old college buddy of mine, and I'm guessing he's the guard," Jimmy said, clamping his hand on the shoulder of his polar opposite in every physical way.

"That's nice, but what I really want to know is why in the hell you weren't here protecting Levi!" Clar jabbed Clint in the chest, her shock having worn off, and anger in its place. He might be sneaky but that wouldn't stop someone from walking in the door and blasting Levi.

Jacki strolled in with determination in her step and a pissed off look on her face. "There's supposed to be...well, I see Mr. Johnny on the Spot has arrived. He totally fits the description Rusty just gave me. Arrogant. Hot. Well built. It's the good cop part that I find hard to believe."

Clar took note of the sarcasm echoing in Jacki's words. There was something else there as well, some undercurrent Clar couldn't quite define.

"I had to take a piss, damn it. I was right there." Clint pointed to the bathroom in the room. "You weren't exactly quiet as a church mouse when you all came in. What with the lady yelling at the nurse and all."

Clar felt like crawling into a hole, embarrassed, her body a mass of shriveling bones and skin because indeed she'd been raising her voice.

"What was he supposed to do Clar, pee in the waste basket?" Jimmy shook his head, then wrapped an arm around her. She didn't need his presence to know she'd blown up for no reason, and she certainly didn't need his comfort either.

"Doing the job you were hired to do would have been a great place to start," Jacki commented, taking a protective position near Levi. "How quick can you pull it out, piss, shake it off, and put it back in before someone would have had you trapped in the bathroom and finished what they'd started at the studio? You have a partner to step in when you need to relieve yourself, where is he?"

"My partner left the room when I came out," Clint snapped back, sizing Jacki up.

"Ah, the nurse. Now it all makes sense. You always were one hell of a poker player." Jimmy chuckled then slapped Clint on the back. "Clint Mason meet Jackson Wolfe, Clar's friend and partner in crime solving."

"Clint Mason. I recall a Texas Ranger by that name whose partner was killed during a cattle rustling bust." Jacki raised an eyebrow and took a step forward, flexing her hands as she stood toe-to-toe with Clint. "I don't believe in coincidences, Mason, do you?"

"Some wannabe PI named after a washed-up movie star pretending to be a cowboy, I presume Ms. Wolfe?" Clint tucked his thumbs into his pants pockets and rocked back on his heels. "Didn't a Jackson Wolfe lose his ranch and prize stud in a poker game?"

"Yes, he did. My father lost it to me." Jacki stood firmly planted, her hands balled up into fists. "I bet I could beat you too."

"Do you really need to do this here? We've got to figure out what happened, cuz I'm sure Cameron knows more than he's saying." Jimmy suggested with a bit of urgency in his words.

Clar hoped a fight wouldn't break out when Jimmy stood between the two, fists clinched tight, praying one of them didn't try to hog tie the other one yet. It was only too clear Jimmy's old college buddy was territorial; she didn't expect it from Jacki. If they played their cards right Clint could be a fount of information, if Jacki didn't rub him the wrong way. Things were more tenuous than either of them knew. Clint wasn't your average cop.

"I got this," Jimmy said softly. "Why don't you go grab a coffee and maybe a sandwich while Clint and I have a chat?"

She didn't want to go, didn't want to trust him with this, but she nodded.

"Come on, Jacki, let's take a walk before there's more horse shit flung around. Jimmy, please take care of this by the time we get back." Clar guided Jacki into the hall.

❦

Jimmy waited for the sound of stomping boots to fade away. The implications were clear—if he didn't deal with this, she and Jacki would.

He partially closed the door, shutting out the possibility of being overheard. When it came to keeping things confidential, he knew that anyone could be lurking in the hallway waiting for a juicy tidbit of information...including Clar and Jacki. "Okay, level with me, Clint, what do you know about this anyway? Why would a former undercover agent Texas Ranger be in the room of a beaten-up porn star?"

"Jimmy, you know the deal. My ass would be hung out to dry by the people who hired me if I told you. I never know who it is that needs my services. I get called, do the job, and get paid. Done deal."

"Bullshit, this is personal." Jimmy knew rules got broken every day.

"Yeah, I could see that," Clint said, looking at the door.

Jimmy stood firm knowing he was showing more of his cards than he should. "So."

"Maybe you should back away from her. Okay, but don't shoot the messenger." Clint widened his stance going into full cop mode. "This goes deep, way deep. There's information that can't get into the hands of the press, and that includes you. There's an investigation going on and we won't know anything until Andres comes out of the coma."

"Fair enough, for now." Jimmy paced, tapping the notebook with a pen. "When did Cameron show up? What's his connection with LAPD?" Clint knew more and Jimmy wanted that information. Starting with Cameron could be a good move.

"I know what you're doing, Jimmy. Let's cut to the chase. Cameron has been investigating the death of that young porn star who was strung up and murdered during a BDSM filming. He's been here for about six months. Just showed up, took up residence, and has been throwing his weight around." Clint stepped over to the door, pulled it open the rest of the way, and looked down the hall. "Just so you know, someone in Jackson Wolfe's camp hired me."

"Holy shit."

CHAPTER 5

"I'm sorry, honey. Didn't mean to run into you young girls." Evie wobbled on her cane looking at the pretty young woman with the spiked hair. She smiled, then glanced toward the wall reaching out for support. *The bitch goes natural and gets better looking. How in the hell does she do it?* "I'm looking for a friend and may have gotten off on the wrong floor." She patted her gray hair.

"Do you want me to help you to the nurse's station to find your friend's room?" The tall redhead in fitted jeans and cowboy boots reached out to steady her teetering.

What is her name? She looks familiar in an old Hollywood kind of way. I can picture her in an old time western. Hmm. She'll be one to keep my eye on as well.

Evie stayed bent over, giving the appearance of suffering from osteoporosis or arthritis. She smiled sweetly, her aged wrinkles crinkling around eyes darting back and forth, reflecting none of her thoughts.

"Thank you, but I prefer to stay independent, miss. Keeps me sharp as a tack." She patted the cowgirl's hand cupping an elbow, wishing she could steal away the beauty the woman probably took for granted. Her own mother had been drop-dead gorgeous in a Marilyn Monroe way, but Evelyn Dagmyer had been blessed with her father's classic 1930's mobster looks. He would have fit in Warner Brother's murderer's row perfectly. Sal DeLuca was not Pretty Boy Floyd by any stretch of the imagination, but he always got even with his enemies.

What had been omitted from her gene pool in the looks department, thanks to Daddy Dearest, Evie made up for in her craftiness, talent, and determination. She could teach the CAS makeup department a thing or two if they'd asked her. Of course they hadn't, that wasn't her function, she was just supposed to answer the phones. She'd learned to deal with beauties like these in her teen years. She'd gotten her share of men at bar time when dressed the part—sexy clothes, false eyelashes, makeup, wigs—a bit of deception in the wee hours of the night coupled with too many cocktails and she'd be twisted in their sheets.

Sex was sex after all. Love and acceptance—they were something totally different. Entities foreign to Evie as getting the credit she was due. Well, her time in the spotlight was coming.

Even though she longed to be recognized for her intelligence, talent, sexuality, and her inner beauty no one seemed interested. No, she'd been passed over for the lack of it her entire life. Humph! Fat chance of it changing as long as worthless women like Clar Turner and her friend continued to tempt the men she so desperately wanted. She should have known when she'd talked to the slut this morning that she'd come a running. Loyal little Clar, beloved by her CAS family, all but one of course.

Men like Dylan Cameron had sung her praises.

He'd all but laughed in her face when she approached him with an idea for a new film, sort of a beauty and the beast in reverse where she'd come out a goddess. Of course, the stars would have been the two of them. Dylan insisted he wasn't into "charity" cases, and mercy fucks.

Much as she'd been tempted to, she hadn't played her ace in the hole card. She was too smart for that. Daddy Dearest had made it perfectly clear when he shipped her to the west coast, she was to remain silent about who she was or she'd lose her allowance, the lush apartment, and the meager trinkets he sent on her birthday and holidays.

Hell, even Levi turned Evie down flat. Granted, he was gay, but he didn't even want to do a film with her even though she'd begged. The memory of that was so humiliating. Said he just wasn't into women. Well, hells bells, if he could fake it with a female co-star why couldn't he with her? Why couldn't he give her that glimmer of fame? Of hope? Well, she'd gotten her justice after all.

"Miss Jackson Wolfe, are you coming or not?" Clar flashed a smile, then went off down the hallway signaling for her companion to follow. The sight of hips swaying followed by the looks from the hospital staff as they passed them sent her stomach lurching. She glared at the bitches walking down the hall, supremely confident, sure of themselves, in a way she never would be. Clar Turner, aka Kandi Kyses. Her mere name crossing her mind churned her blood into a boiling frenzy. Sooner or later, the queen of smut would get what was coming to her. Fate would make it so just like it had for Levi. She was just like her daddy, her enemies always paid. She couldn't wait for it to happen. She lived for that day. The sooner the better as far as she was concerned.

"Stupid girls." Evie brushed away the warmth Jackson Wolfe's hand had left behind on her skin, gloating as she processed the information. She'd heard the former PI was in town helping Clar with Levi. Too bad the piss ant Levi hadn't died right there on the studio floor along with the rest of them. It would have been one less thorn in her side.

Lingering a moment, she slipped closer to the ajar door to Levi's room, hoping to listen in on the hunk and Jimmy O'Brien, gathering information. Nobody passing by as much as glanced at her, why should they, no one ever noticed her.

"I know what you're thinking Jimmy. Reed Cameron is Dylan Cameron's uncle...."

Icy fear spread through her like frostbite at the words. Oh my god, why hadn't she put his connection with Dylan together before now? A chill went through her. Detective Reed Cameron had been one of her father's many henchmen. This couldn't be good. He'd been the one who'd followed Sal DeLuca's orders to stash Evie and her mother—former lounge singer Belle Anderson—far from Chicago. He'd planted them in a small northern Wisconsin town where life was unforgiving for an ugly girl and her mother whom everyone knew was a mobster's girl. Oh sure, daddy dear had made sure they had plenty of food, money, clothes, but not one ounce of love for his "ugly duckling" daughter.

Being so obsessed with Levi she'd not put Dylan and the detective together. She thought the cop was in LA to keep an eye on her. Now it could be otherwise. She wobbled down the hall to the elevators, ducking into the bathroom to ditch the old lady getup.

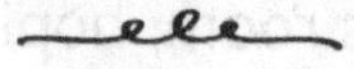

Reed Cameron stepped into the crowded elevator staring at the door as it closed. He wasn't in the mood to deal with morons and their sniffling. He had a victim to check on and questions to get the answers to after Clar Turner walked out on him in the middle of questioning. It boiled his blood remembering the snickering of the officers when she and the redhead took a hike. He had no real reason to hold her and it pissed him off that she wasn't intimidated by him in the least. He'd need that edge to get anything done in this town.

Since his rookie days, he'd witnessed a lot of deaths patrolling the streets of Chicago. Including those he'd turned a blind eye to as a detective. Those days were behind him the moment his sister's son had been brutally murdered. He'd fulfill the promise he'd made to her as they placed Dylan into the ground.

He'd find the killer and serve justice the only way he knew how...with a Glock.

The deal Cameron had made with Sal was that he'd watch out for his LA investments, if he was released of his Chicago duties to the DeLuca family. So, he packed up his life and moved to the west coast after landing a position at the LAPD. While California had the beaches and sunshine, the crime in the streets wasn't much different. Brutal. Deadly. Senseless. Tragic.

Cameron smoothed the permanent wrinkles of his suit and ran a hand through his thinning gray hair. The elevator slid to a stop and he stepped onto the floor as a non-descript woman bustled into a car going down. *Evelyn Dagmyer, the receptionist? What in the hell would she be doing here? She'd been damned near hysterical this morning at CAS. Nah, it can't be her*, he told himself as the door whooshed closed.

He pushed the woman from his mind and swaggered down the hall to Levi's room keeping his eyes on his surroundings. While he certainly didn't agree with the victim's lifestyle, he needed to keep him alive to find out what he remembered in the studio. Any little tidbit of information could lead him to the killer now being dubbed the Porn Star Slayer by the local press. Personally, he'd just as soon toss all the reporters into the ocean with an anchor wrapped around their necks. He'd gotten rid of O'Brien once, he could do it again, if he had to.

Cameron slid open the door to Levi Andres' room and stopped cold. Jimmy O'Brien and a guy he didn't recognize gathered at the end of the hospital bed; their voices barely audible.

"What the hell, O'Brien," Cameron hissed, curbing his desire to throw Jimmy and the lean, dangerous looking shield of a man out the door. "How'd you get in here? And who the hell are you?" He glared at the second man. "And where's the protection detail I assigned?" He waited, mulling over how he could use these two to his advantage. "Never mind, I would bet that Clar Turner and the redhead have something to do with you being here." He'd been looking for an excuse to haul her in and this was a beauty.

Jimmy's lip curled up, sending Cameron's blood pressure to an all new high. It wasn't enough that he had to deal with a murder that may be connected to his nephew. Unlike the Chicago incident years ago, he couldn't threaten the reporter with a reliable witness present. Instead, now he had to play all tit-ty-finger nice, or better yet, smart. Maybe the time had come for him to start working with rather than against O'Brien. O'Brien's investigative skills, while a bit rusty, were the best he'd ever seen; he could be a valued asset.

"Detective, nice to see you too." Jimmy turned from Reed dismissively. "This is Clint Mason. He's been hired by Jackson Wolfe to watch over Levi until Clar can get him out of here, and far from this cancerous city. As for your protection detail, it seems they never showed up."

What the fuck? Fury went through him as he thought of his direct orders being ignored. The local cops didn't hold him in high esteem so he'd guess he shouldn't be surprised but it still pissed him off. Hell, maybe he needed these two clowns. Cameron sized up the hired body-guard, assessing him from his unwavering gaze to the way he held his ground. "Former cop, Mason?"

"Yes, sir. Texas Ranger to be exact." Clint moved closer to Levi's bed, his protective stance sending a clear message—don't try it or you're dead. "I know who you are, Detective Reed Cameron, and your connection to the Chicago DeLuca Family."

"Humph, didn't realize it wasn't common knowledge all law enforcement had some kind of relationship with criminals in our city,"

Cameron snickered, slithering closer to Levi's bed and the man guarding him. "Is that all it takes to be a big Texas Ranger; a bit of common knowledge?" He sensed there was more there, for a man his age to be a former anything spoke of a murky past. And it seemed that he and O'Brien were pals a bit interesting.

"There's a difference between working with a criminal that's a snitch and being on a crime boss's payroll." The former cowboy cop reached him within seconds, his jaw clinched so tight he thought he could hear him grinding his teeth. Cameron glanced down and smiled at the balled fist twitching at Mason's side. He'd hit paydirt. Maybe he hadn't lost his touch after all.

"Clint, speaking from experience, this scum bag isn't worth the effort." Jimmy stepped between Cameron and Mason, cutting the slight thread of intimidation Cameron wove between them.

"Hey, Houston! We have a problem here." Dangling from Clar Turner's hands were a disheveled grey wig and a rickety walking cane. "We found these in the women's bathroom just down the hall. They were shoved into the trash can."

Cameron knew in an instant. It was Evie who'd slipped into the elevator.

"Clar."

"Shhh, everyone, be quiet a moment!" Clar looked around the room until her gaze swept onto Levi. Leaning over Levi, her ear mere inches from his lips, Clar could have sworn she heard her name.

"Clar." His breath a light whisper that only a butterfly would feel.

Tears streamed down her face as she clung to his hand. She pulled up a chair, leaning in closer to Levi and pressed the call button. "Shhh, you need your strength."

Levi licked his parched lips, a tiny bit of a smile edging them. "You are my strength."

"Clear the area, please. I need to check his vitals." The doctor strolled through the door, his words gentle and commanding at the same time. "I'll let you know when you can come back in."

Clar smiled, squeezing his hand again, then gently kissed his forehead. "I'll be right back."

"You're a very lucky man, Mr. Andres."

Clar and the rest of them left the room to allow the doctor to do his job. Levi was alive! In her mind, the biggest hurdle had just been crossed. Fate was not going to take another person she loved and cared for, not this time, not while there was breath in her body.

"As soon as the doctor comes back out, I'm going in there to question him." Cameron pulled out a small notebook and pen, his warning glance sweeping over them as they huddled in the hallway. "I want no interference at all. I want you all to stay out here. I don't want anyone influencing his words."

"If you think for one minute I'm letting you alone with him you are absolutely out of your mind!" Clar hissed, her back facing Levi's room, guarding it from the dragon waiting to light it on fire.

"Clar," Jacki touched her arm, and she jerked it away, "let's wait and see what the doctor has to say. It might just be that no one can go in there at all. Levi might be off limits even to you."

"No, I'm all the family he has." Clar's heart sank into the rolling of her stomach.

"We all know that, but the medical staff doesn't." Jimmy's voice sent soothing calmness over the fear and rage trying to take over. She fell into his waiting arms, allowing his strength to protect her. It wasn't until Levi said her name that it hit her how much pain he must have endured. How much punishment had been delivered to his mind and body.

The doctor stepped out into the hall. "He's doing well with all things considered. At this point it doesn't appear as if there's been any brain damage, but the emotional damage may take months, years even, to repair." The doctor turned to Clar, a smile on his face. "Ms. Turner, Levi is asking for you."

Clar took a step toward the door with Cameron hot on her heels. "I'm sorry, I'll only allow Ms. Turner in at this time."

"I need to question the victim as to what he remembers. It's vital to the case."

"I understand that, but it's not going to happen today." The doctor's warning left no room for argument.

"Alright, I'll do it your way." Cameron reached into his pocket, pulling out a small tape player holding it out to Clar. "Ms. Turner, get what you can out of him. I'll talk with you when you're finished."

"No promises. It'll depend on Levi." Clar took the small recorder with no intention of using it, and stole cautiously into the room.

"Levi?" Clar pulled a chair next to the bed, taking a hold of his hand. He looked so weak, and helpless. Like a sick child she supposed. And like a mother she wanted to protect him.

"Clar." His eyes fluttered for a moment, then opened, a smile seeping on his lips. "Dead on me. Filming. Kicking me."

"Shhh." His words sparked an idea. Clar didn't begin to fight the tears spilling down her cheeks. "There's plenty of time for all that. You are alive, that's all that matters. Quiet now and get some rest, we'll talk more tomorrow."

Levi squeezed her hand with a force she didn't expect. "Wrappers. Kandi Kisses." Levi's eyes fluttered closed.

Clar kissed his forehead then walked into the hall. She wrapped herself in Jimmy's arms, shaking with what Levi had told her. Taking a deep breath, she looked over at Cameron weighing her next words.

"There is something that needs to be checked out. It may be nothing, but important enough for Levi to say it before he fell asleep." She faced Cameron holding Jimmy's hand. Jacki and Clint flanked them, enforcing her defense.

"And that would be, Ms. Turner?"

"I have a condition first, and one that I know goes against the right way to investigate. But then you've never been one to do it the honest way anyhow, have you?"

"That was a long time ago, in a life I've left behind."

"I'm not so sure, but at any rate here's my condition. After I tell you what Levi said, you have to take us on any of your investigations. Deal?"

Cameron shifted for a moment. "It's that important to you to break the law for?"

"Yes."

"Deal."

Clar sighed with relief, then took a step toward Cameron. "Levi only said words. Words that I feel are important enough to check out. We need to get our hands on that film from the day of the murders. If it was running, we'll have more than enough to figure out who is behind this."

CHAPTER 6

Jimmy's Beach
House

The sun, a bright orange ball on the line of the horizon, cast a beautiful eerie hue on the waves of the Pacific Ocean. Despite the wonder of dusk, Clar couldn't shake the image of the old lady, wig, and cane from her mind. Why would someone come disguised into a hospital and lurk outside Levi's room? She should have paid closer attention. She should have really looked at the woman before hurrying down the hall.

"So just what are you suggesting?" Jimmy's voice bounced around the room. Clar focused on the reflections in the window of Jacki and Clint sitting behind her on the sandy-white couch while Jimmy paced in front of them. "There is no way I'm going along with that plan. No way! Clar's not going back into the business! Damn it, Clar could be next on the maniac's hit list."

"Are you even listening, O'Brien? You're as pigheaded today as you were years ago." Jacki shook her head and leaned back into the sofa. "You haven't heard a word we said, have you?"

"All I hear is that you want Clar to go back into that world. A world she's fought so hard to leave behind. Do you honestly realize how hard that was for her?" Jimmy stopped his pacing and plopped onto a red bar stool at the breakfast bar. "Do you?"

"Probably more than you do as I was around to pick up the pieces after you hounded her," Jacki accused, her words laced with arsenic.

Clar winced because it was true and then saw Jimmy's guilty look. Damn, she didn't want it to be like this, she didn't want to get back into skin flicks either, but if it would mean catching Levi's attacker and stopping him before he hurt anyone else, she'd do it.

"Ah, excuse me but I'm standing right here and I can speak for myself." Clar leaned against the back of a stool near Jimmy, and glared at them all. "Jacki and Clint, it would have been better if you'd let me in on your plans but I understand your need for expediency." At Jimmy's snort she turned to spear him with a repressive look. "And as for you, O'Brien, I'm not some lovelorn little waif you have to worry about, and I make my own decisions. I think they're right; we need someone on the inside at CAS, and that someone is me."

"Like hell. If someone has to go in, it's going to be me." Jimmy stood with his hands planted on his waist, his blazing gaze scorching everyone in its path. "They want you to go undercover, Clar. To go back to the studio and start filming again."

"I admit you're sexy enough but you don't have the qualifications." Clar chuckled, hoping to release some of the tension the conversation had brought to what should have been a beautiful and peaceful setting.

"I don't fucking care. If CAS is hard up, they will take me. They want you to be in the direct line of this deranged person." His whiskey eyes flickered with concern and something Clar had never seen in them before. Fear.

"Give us a little credit, O'Brien, we have a plan," Jacki said.

Ignoring Jimmy and his tantrum, Clar gazed out to the ocean. She understood Jimmy's fear, hell the thought scared the daylights out of her too, not that she was about to admit it. It really wasn't that bad of an idea, but.... If she continued to hide and live in fear of being exposed, what kind of life could she really have? "Is that all there is, me going back in front of the lens again? We don't know what is on that film yet. We don't know what my candy has to do with this, if anything."

"How do we know Cameron hasn't gone back on his word? We've got to have a plan, Clar." Jacki came up behind her, placing a hand on her shoulder. "I'd never put you in danger. Clint came up with the plan and I agree with him as long as we are there with you. Besides, Max would never forgive me if he didn't get to try to steal your chocolates anymore."

"Thank God for Max. I always did like that horse of yours." Clar turned, catching the sharp glint of worry in Jacki's eye. Sighing, Clar turned back to the peace of the ocean, sensing the dangers lurking in its depths. "What's this plan of yours?"

Jacki and Clint explained how they'd go in undercover to make sure she had protection. Clint would take on the role of cameraman, putting him directly in the studio. Jacki would be out front with Evie, checking out customers as they came in and keeping an eye on her.

Jimmy glared at the three of them. "I can't believe you're still gonna do this. What do you do about Evelyn then? She may not look it, but that woman knows everything that goes on in the studio. Plus, she knows me, has no love lost for Clar and, besides, I'm not about to let you that far out of my sight."

If Clar could bore a hole through Jimmy's stubborn brain, she would gladly do so. She understood his fear for her, and somewhere deep inside it melted that little bit of anger toward him, but she would not be controlled. "You're either part of the solution, Jimmy, or you're part of the problem, which is it going to be? I can make my own decisions and decide what is or what isn't good for me."

"You've worked too damn hard to leave that life, and now you want to enter the lion's den not looking at all like Kandi Kyses, by the way. Not to mention doing so will blow your entire new life to shreds."

She'd grown soft, put on a few pounds, and his comment stung. "No, you did that when you announced it on SXY this morning." She wanted to call the words back the minute he blanched. Instead, the look he gave her spoke volumes increasing the distance between them. He turned on his heel and walked out the door.

"Oh shit," Jacki said.

"Yeah, he's got it pretty bad," Clint chirped in, a smile lurking at the corner of his mouth.

"He's an overbearing SOB I can't seem to pull from my side." Clar watched Jimmy stomped down the steps and onto the sandy beach. Her heart flipped thinking she'd finally succeeded in pushing him away—for good this time. Her soul cried instead of cheering for joy.

"While that may be true, he's always loved you. What's so bad about letting him in?" Jacki put an arm around Clar's shoulder, hugging her ever so slightly. "Giving him a morsel of consideration would go a long way."

Clar's heart softened with a tiny sigh. It wouldn't do any harm to be nice to him, but nothing more. Not yet. At least not until this business of finding who assaulted Levi was done.

What the hell had she done? Clar was moving before she could talk herself out of it. Yeah, they had their differences but she couldn't let things end this way.

Jimmy strode down the beach wishing he had a wall he could kick, something he could flatten, because he felt just as damned guilty as he ought to. Clar didn't trust him, she sure as hell didn't want his help. Leaving seemed like the best option but he knew he couldn't, not really.

What a fucking mess. Clar Turner was the love of his life. He knew it the first time he'd done a news report on one of her films. Under all the bleached blonde hair, fake tan, and makeup lay the woman he was destined to be with.

She had been as broken as he was back then. Maybe that's what bonded them at first before it all turned to shit.

Both of Clar's parents were killed in a tragic accident, no family and nowhere to go, Levi Andres became her savior and Dylan her friend. If only Jimmy had been there first, maybe she wouldn't be in this current situation. Fuck, maybe she flat out wouldn't be in this position because Jimmy wouldn't have encouraged her to get into the skin business like they had.

Even if she hated him, even if she walked away from him in the end, he'd do what he had to in order to protect her. No way would he lose her to a maniac killer. The hair brained idea of Wolfe's and Mason's didn't sit well with him. The whole thing should be handled by Cameron and his cronies, not a former film star and her PI friend with a washed-up Texas Ranger and disgraced reporter as sidekicks.

"Jimmy!" Clar's voice filtered through the soft crashes of the waves along the shoreline. "Jimmy, wait."

A seismic shift went through him at her voice, stopping him in his tracks, and he started to hope again. And then realized he only heard one set of racing footsteps. Her safety detail wasn't even protecting her. Shit. The last remnants of the sun's rays barely lit the horizon. This could be the most dangerous time of the evening on the beach for anyone alone. Jimmy swore under his breath and turned toward Clar as she ran through the sand.

His heart hammered in his chest. A vision of Pamela Anderson in that lifeguard movie, jogging on the beach in a red one-piece swimsuit flashed through his mind. Only it was Clar and every bit as sexy, if not more because it was real, because she was his. He pulled at his shorts, adjusting the discomfort there.

Clar pulled up, huffing, and puffing to catch her breath. "Geez, I've forgotten what it's like to run through the sand. I guess you're right about me being out of shape."

"Nah, I was being an asshole. It suits you, more real somehow, like I could hold you." *Yeah, real smooth, idiot.*

She gave him a funny look.

Jimmy waited a moment longer before turning to walk further along the beach. He was careful to keep her between him and the water in hopes that any SOB who might be watching from the cliffs wouldn't get a clear shot at them with the setting sun in their eyes. As soon as he got her to his secret cove, he'd feel better. He'd been heading there to think but now it was a perfect place to get her alone. A group of boulders several yards from the beach house offered the perfect sanctuary from the day's troubles.

"Right." She came up beside him, nudging him with an elbow. Jimmy smiled; thankful she didn't appear to be angry with him any longer. "What I can't live with is you trying to run my life...still. I'm not that scared little girl any more, Jimmy, with my father's conspiracy theory and list. I've grown up and moved on from that life, my parents' deaths, and away from the California lifestyle. I don't want it back, but if going back in front of the camera will entice the murderer then I'll do it. All this senseless killing has to stop."

"I agree but you need to let the professionals handle it. Hell, it's what cops sign on for." Jimmy sat on the sand, leaning against one of the boulders. The tide was low and the ocean lightly crashed the shore. Perfect for a romantic rendezvous, He patted the sand by his side and relaxed when she sat next to him, and placed a hand over his.

"You know we can't trust Cameron with this."

"I know. Don't think I'm not scared because I am. I know the risk and the chances of me coming out the same person are little to none. But can't you see I have to do this?" She paused a moment as the waves sloshed the shore then sighed deeply. "I feel there's no choice, if putting my life at risk could stop the killings and save others, then I have to do it."

Jimmy pulled Clar to him and scrutinized her hazel eyes, searching for anything that would give him what he needed to convince her to abandon the plan. His gaze travelled down to her lips, a natural rose color begging to be kissed. The tip of her tongue snaked out and his control washed out with the waves.

—◦◦◦—

The last thing she planned on was being in Jimmy's arms. But here she was, nestled on the sand beside some boulders with him gazing down at her. The damn organ that pumped blood into a living body jack-hammered against her chest. Heat surged through her body. Clar wrapped her arms around his neck and offered her lips without hesitation. She needed this bliss, this healing, and whether he wanted to admit it or not so did he.

"Clar, I can't..." Jimmy's finger traced her lower lip, singeing the sensitive area. Hot liquid gold glided from the spot to the mounting pressure at the valley between her thighs.

"Just shut up and kiss me." Clar pulled him down, tasting him for the first time. Her body exploded in a fiery blaze of desire.

She moaned into him, pleading for more than humanly possible. It had been a long time since Clar felt the warmth of a man. The fact that she'd chosen Jimmy was a surprise. Life threw a curve ball straight into a well thought out life and landed between the attack on Levi and her assault on Jimmy's mouth.

Clar wanted to hit it out of the ballpark for a home run.

"Jimmy..." His name slipped off her tongue like silk, and she shivered in heated need.

Light as a feather, his hand glazed over a breast, sending another shot of craving into her fluttering belly. Jimmy's eyes smoldered with intensity, and Clar licked suddenly parched lips. Clar needed his touch encompassing her entire body...inside and out.

She wanted to feel what making love with him was like, before her life disappeared.

Warm lips found their way to the sweet spot on her neck, then travelled the path to a sensitive earlobe. Hot breath mingled with the fresh scent of sand and surf, sending all circuits into overdrive. Every muscle in her body tensed with heat and trembled with cold.

"Clar," Jimmy whispered into her ear, fanning a strand of hair lightly across the lobe. "I've waited a long time to become one with you, and believe me, my body is letting me know just what that would mean. I just can't, not this way. Not in a heated rush."

"But..." Tears welled threatening to burst, and Clar took a deep breath calming the quaking realization of his words. "...we may not have another opportunity, Jimmy."

"That, my dear, is not an option. I plan on ravaging your body a hundred times over once this ordeal is over and the son-of-a-bitch is in prison."

"I've been such a fool, Jimmy, in not trusting you." Clar snuggled deep into his arms, letting the tears fall freely. Her tilted axes felt to have shifted back a bit more in their world. Together they just might have a chance in this life.

The two bodies groping each other in the sand turns my stomach into convulsions. Damn, I wish I could see better. Trust the bastard reporter to choose a rocky fortress for his sex on the beach. It's a wonder they don't get sand crabs or something. Humph! The porn queen has returned and taken up where she left off, in the arms of some unsuspecting man. Kandi Kyses may have changed her appearance, but a leopard can't change their spots. She's still the whore and the reason I had to kill Dylan. Her and the entourage at the studio all had to die.

Too bad there hadn't been enough time to make sure the homo had died as well. Although if he had, the message wouldn't have been relayed, so I guess I did good there. Besides, I knew she'd come running for her friend. The pink candy wrapper wasn't enough to bring her back here. Didn't count on the former PI bringing in a hired gun though. Just another body to contend with.

And that's exactly what will happen...everyone will be contended with. One way or another. Just how and when to do it?

CHAPTER 7

Jimmy glanced down at the small hand his fingers wrapped around. An hour ago, he wouldn't have given his chances of having Clar next to him a snowball's chance in hell. Now she walked alongside him as the sun set over the California beach. It wasn't much to the average Joe, but to Jimmy these past few moments with Clar made him feel like he'd just won the lottery. He wouldn't let some evil thug steal them from him, from them.

The lights from his beach house illuminated the sandy path to the porch, as well as his house guests. "Look, Clar," he chuckled, pointing at the two with their heads together. "It seems Jacki and Clint have become friends."

"A former Ranger and a PI instructor turned horse rancher, I'm sure they are plotting their way right into solving..." Clar stopped short, and looked up, letting out a little gasp. "I guess I'm not the only one ignoring their duty. At least someone's keeping their priorities straight."

She slipped her hand from his. "For a moment..."

"It felt like everything was normal." Jimmy finished for her. The knowledge of danger had been pushed to the back of his mind but not forgotten. "That we were just two lovers strolling on the beach." His heart broke for both of them. The danger now glowed like a beacon in the night, signaling what lay waiting ahead.

Jimmy took her in his arms, holding her close. "Friends, Clar. You're with friends who love and care for you, and Levi." Her body trembled with sobbing against his chest and he held her until she calmed. "Come, it's getting a bit chilly. We should see just what Jacki and Clint have cooked up for us."

Jimmy peered toward a shadowy figure lurking around the house window. "Stay here," he whispered, then took off at a jog through the sand. "Hey!" he hollered, slipping, and sliding, as he worked his way through the depth of the grains.

"Jimmy!"

Clar's voice reached him as he dove onto the porch. His outstretched hand barely missed the ankle slipping back into the shadows. "Damn it!" Gasping for air, Jimmy rolled onto his back. A large, black shadow blanketed him. Jimmy sprung to his feet, and raised his fists in defense.

"Damn, O'Brien, you need to put numbers on this damn place of yours. I've combed the entire shore looking for you." Cameron stepped from the shadows, hands raised, palms open. "Hold on there, cowboy, I come in peace."

Jimmy released his clamped fingers, slowly and one at a time, senses on high alert. The devil stood on his deck proclaiming to come in peace. Jimmy knew of some prime swampland for sale if anyone believed Cameron.

"What the hell are you doing lurking around in the dark? You've got no business spying on me or my guests. There's this new way of communicating, it's called the cell phone with the capability of either actually calling a person or texting, you know, typing a message. Use it next time you decide to become a Peeping Tom!" Jimmy bopped down the steps, eager to reach

Clar. He needed her level head to keep him from busting Cameron in the mouth.

—*ele*—

Clar reached out for Jimmy's arm, halting him from stomping out to shore. "What does Cameron want?" Clar whispered, sucking in a nervous breath. The menacing figure stood on the porch as if waiting to snatch its prey at any moment.

This couldn't be good. A detective on the front porch. At night. Unannounced. Had Levi taken a turn for the worst? Clar wasn't ready to go down that road. Not yet. Not before she got to talk with him one last time. Not before she found out who put him in the hospital after leaving him for dead.

"I don't know, nor do I care. The man's a snake that crawls out when you least expect it." Jimmy hissed, glancing over her shoulder. "I've felt that bite once, I don't plan on doing so again."

"Then don't give him a reason, Jimmy." Clar leaned in closer, kissing him. "Please. We may need his help." She gazed into his eyes, relieved to see some of the darkness of tension subside. But suspicion remained locked into his defenses. "Besides, he may have some information we could use. Can you put your differences aside, for Levi?"

"Do you know how you subdue a snake? By the back of his head, and that's exactly what I plan on doing." Jimmy looked past her shoulder. There was a deep hatred lingering there, one that could ruin everything if he didn't rein it in.

Taking his hand, they turned toward the beach house. Cameron stood at the top of the steps like a soldier waiting to make his next move.

"It's a bit late for a call, isn't it, Detective?" Clar called out as she made her way through the sandy beach. "I'm sure it's not for social reasons, or am I mistaken?"

"Actually, it's you I've come to talk with. After all, we never did get a chance at the precinct the other day before you stormed out. You're damn lucky I didn't have you arrested." Cameron glared down at her, his dark, beady eyes menacing. Lurking behind the threatening veil lay a sense of grief Clar was sure he thought hidden away. A surprise discovery she'd let the others in on later. "But that's not why I'm here."

"Well, then I think we should go inside before you come up with some trumped up charge. I'd forgotten how chilly it gets out on the beach once the sun sets. Shall we go in, Jimmy?" With her hand still clasped firmly with Jimmy's, Clar walked into the beach house praying the presence of Jacki and Clint would be enough to keep the two enemies at bay.

"Jacki. Clint. I'm sure you remember Detective Reed Cameron. He's here to talk to me about Levi and what happened at the studio." Clar let Jimmy's hand slip from hers. She hadn't realized she'd been shaking until the security of him was gone. "Detective, would you like something to drink?" she asked, crossing her arms across her chest as the shaking subsided. "I'm sure Jimmy has some water, or iced tea, or even milk if you'd prefer?"

Cameron flipped open his notebook, looking pointedly at Clar. "Um, no thank you. What I do need to know is what your relationship with Levi Andres is. How long have you known him, Ms. Turner?"

I barely got away that time! Stupid, stupid, stupid. If the detective hadn't shown up when he did...well let's just say they'd be rethinking their next move. Ha, they think they are being so clever. Making plans. Who do they think they are? Starsky and Hutch? More like Abbott and Costello. This ain't no Hollywood movie and I ain't no Hollywood movie villain. She'll find out just how real soon enough. I just need to stay on top of their plans. Stay one step ahead of them.

CHAPTER 8

"I've known Levi since I was in my early twenties. Why?" Clar took a deep breath. She really didn't want to open old wounds. She'd been living in a state of shock and despair when Levi came to her rescue. The hurt and pain of those years following the death of her parents were long buried, giving way to peace and acceptance. It all seemed to be slipping away and that scared the hell out of her.

"How did you meet? Pardon my lack of knowledge in how things work in Hollywood, but it seems unlikely someone like you would become friends with a person in the adult film business." Cameron remained standing, his pencil gliding across the pad. Clar found it odd that in this day of handheld electronic technology; he didn't use his phone or tablet to make notes.

"Strange bed fellows sometimes make the best of friends, as I'm sure you are well aware of, Cameron." Jimmy moved next to Clar. She was grateful for his presence next to her. Until recently, Levi, Jacki, and Jimmy were the only people who knew of her unstable past—and her supposedly anonymous new life. A life that was about to be revealed to those who cared enough to listen. Her new friends and clients didn't know about her past. Of course that would all change now. It saddened Clar to think she may lose everything she'd worked for all because of some evil doer with vengeance on their mind, but didn't deter her from the chosen path. Cameron was after her for a reason and it behooved all of them to pay attention.

"I'll get to you later, O'Brien." Cameron glared at Jimmy with a hatred Clar had never witnessed before. There was probably a lot more between them than Jimmy had let on. Definitely a history there, but what could cause such contempt for each other? A woman? No, she didn't think so. She would have known by now.

Regardless, there certainly wasn't a love affair with those two bull-headed men. She touched Jimmy's hand to show unity, hoping to calm the waters.

Cameron sneered and wrote in his book. "Ms. Turner, I'll get straight to the point. Where were you the night of the murders?"

"At my home, in Wisconsin, making chocolate bunnies. You know the kind that the kiddos love to eat the ears off of on Easter. I'm sure you'll recall me calling the studio right after and Evie crying crocodile tears until you took the phone."

"Yeah, the poor kid, she was really upset."

"Poor kid," Clar murmured, shocked. No one ever thought of the obnoxious receptionist in those terms. She shared a startled look with Jacki.

Cameron glared at her.

"Damn best chocolate in the world, I might add," Jacki remarked, winking at Clar, making Cameron turn his glare on her.

"Doesn't prove anything. The call came from a cell. You could've been anywhere when you made it."

She could hardly believe the accusation. He had to know it wasn't true, didn't he? Cameron continued watching her, as if waiting for her to break. Well, he didn't know her at all if he thought that was going to happen. He was like a shark in the water trying to scare up dinner.

Damned if she'd let any of her friends go down in the feeding frenzy. "There's a way to triangulate cell signals isn't there, Jacki?"

"Damned straight there is," Jacki said.

Clint nodded.

Jimmy squeezed her hand. "I used it once following—"

"Me," Clar cut in.

"Fine, play it your way. When did you allegedly hear about the attack?" Cameron flipped a page and continued wearing out the lead in his pencil.

"On SXY a few minutes after O'Brien outted me on national TV. Check the tape if you don't believe me." Clar squeezed Jimmy's hand to let him know it was okay. "You know that moment when the old lady in *Titanic* is molding her pottery and she hears the news cast that a diving team has found a portrait of a young woman wearing the 'Heart of the Ocean' and she stops her spinning and walks slowly over to the TV?

"I was molding chocolate bunnies when the breaking news report about the murders at the studio came on. I followed up with a call to the studio to find out if Levi was involved; then one more to Jacki asking her to meet me here in LA."

"Involved? Do you think he orchestrated the entire attack?" The constantly moving pencil ceased its scratching. Cameron's black eyes squinted at her.

"Humph! That's a pretty big word for you, isn't it, Cameron? Orchestrated. Do you even know what it means?" Jimmy huffed, then rubbed his rib where Clar jabbed him with an elbow.

"And can anyone verify your alibi?" Cameron queried, the scratching on the paper increasing.

"How about your alibi, Cameron," Jimmy cut in. "It's pretty damned convenient that you were at the crime scene."

"Chocolate bunnies? Am I a suspect here, detective? And *no*, I don't believe Levi had anything to do with the murders."

"At this point we're still gathering information, Ms. Turner." Cameron kept his eyes on his pad as he flipped back several pages. "What was your connection with Dylan Cameron?"

"What are you getting at here? He was a fellow actor at the studio and a friend. Dylan was really a great guy." She saw his eyes soften and sucked in a breath as it all came together. Cameron? They shared the same last name. Was it possible they were related? "We co-starred in only one film together."

"And his relationship with Mr. Andres?"

"It was a working relationship. Detective, it is no secret Levi is gay. Nor is it a secret that he had a crush on Dylan. If for any reason you think he's involved, I would bark up a different tree," Jacki interjected with a touch of sarcasm.

"Ms. Turner, please ask your friends to pipe down or I'll take you into the precinct for questioning, and our deal will be off," Cameron threatened, his back straightening ram-rod.

"I've got this and I appreciate your protection. I've got nothing to hide, and neither does Levi." Clar glanced at her friends who wanted nothing more than to protect her. "It's true, Levi did have a crush on Dylan. However, Dylan wasn't interested in his advances. And for the record, Levi was devastated when Dylan died."

"Would you say the killing was a crime of passion?" Cameron's gaze, vacant of any passion but filled with sadness, met hers. *Oh god, it was true, there was a link between him and Dylan. What could she say?*

"What the hell does Dylan Cameron's murder have to do with the recent attacks? I'm not following your reason for the line of questioning," Jimmy stammered, suspicion edging his words. "Be careful where you go with this, Cameron—your friends aren't here to protect you."

"How did you meet Mr. Andres, Ms. Turner?" Flipping his notebook closed, Cameron slipped the pad and pencil into a pocket of his suit jacket.

"That is a long and personal story. The short version is after my parents' car accident, Levi literally saved my life." Clar clung to the thread of sanity slipping away.

"When you left Wisconsin the first time."

It seemed he knew her history. Just how far back did this go? She remembered Jimmy's words. "It's not surprising you know, seeing you worked side by side with my father."

Cameron's eyes narrowed. "Yeah, and he wouldn't like you sticking your neck out this way. Take my advice and stick your head back in that candy box, things are gonna get messy."

He stood, nervously adjusting his crumpled suit jacket. Seemed she'd hit a sore spot. "You know my dad wasn't very popular in some circles because he worked internal affairs."

This had to end. She couldn't take much more of opening her life up to scrutiny by this man who carried a badge.

"Hmm, okay, that's all for now, Ms. Turner. I'd advise you to let the police handle this. We could be dealing with a deranged fan." Cameron's gaze scanned the room, pausing for a moment with each set of eyes. "Don't do anything on your own. I'm warning you. Accidents happen all the time, don't they?"

Clar sat there stunned as her world collided. Why would he mention accidents happening when that's how her parents died? Cameron knew something but wasn't saying.

"And just what might that be, Cameron? Actually solve the case?" Jimmy spat back to the detective following him out the door. He didn't trust the man one bit. He couldn't help it; Cameron was a festering wound in his soul but that was kid's stuff compared to what he'd just dropped on Clar. "What'd you have to do with her parents' death?" he said in a deceptively calm tone.

"Not a fucking thing, not that you'll believe me." Cameron turned, his gaze blazing hot. "She needed a shock to keep from doing something stupid and getting hurt, she got it."

The guy knew a lot more than he was saying.

"Just leave it be for now, O'Brien, and stick with the case at hand. You know how the law works. I want to get to the bottom of this as much as any of you do. And if it means putting the lot of you behind bars to do it, I will!" He pulled his shoulders back and puffed out his chest.

"Detective, you certainly must have a suspect." Clint stood, ogling Cameron. If Clint was intimidated by the veteran of the streets, he didn't show it. Jimmy admired Clint for his cool and calm manner, while all he wanted to do was shoot Cameron between the eyes and put him out of his misery.

"As a *former* Texas Ranger, Mason, you know I couldn't divulge that information even if I wanted to." Cameron shook his head, stuffing his hands into his jacket pockets. "I'm not about to give you any information that may send you off on some chase down a rabbit hole."

"He knows something, Clint," Jimmy interjected, walking over to the door leading out to the beach. "He's not saying, and he won't. Even if it's just an inkling, the man who protects people from thugs isn't going to tell you who is or who isn't on his list of suspects. It might have one of his cutthroat buddies scribbled on it." Sarcasm rang in Jimmy's words, and he smiled seeing Cameron bristle at them. It was a small victory to see him squirm. The SOB deserved it for all his years working on the wrong side of the law with the wrong guys.

Cameron glared at everyone in the room before a crooked little smile slipped across his face. "I know you're planning something. Whatever it is, at least let me in on it. It's the only way I'll be able to protect and keep any of you from being the next victim. Meet me at the studio tomorrow at noon. Have a pleasant evening." He nodded, then walked through the door Jimmy held open.

Jimmy followed Cameron out onto the beach. He needed to get a few things straight, like finding out why he was in California. "Cameron!"

The detective paused then turned, a hand slipping to the inside his jacket. "What is it now, O'Brien?"

Jimmy swallowed back the acid taste of bile building in his mouth. As true as his strong dislike for what Cameron stood for, Jimmy needed to know a few things from him and no one else. "Why are you in LA? I can't imagine DeLuca sent you out here to retire in the sand and surf of sunny California."

"Listen, those days in Chicago are in the past and behind me. I paid my dues and I needed a change of scenery. Why not spend the rest of my days soaking in the sun rather than shoveling snow six months of the year?" Cameron smiled briefly, shrugging his shoulders.

"Those days are never in the past. You of all people know you don't just walk away from the mob. Do you take me for a fool?" Just because he was thousands of miles away from the streets of Chicago didn't mean he'd left that life behind. A life Cameron had built on the side of the law which Jimmy tried to destroy the only way he knew how. Uncovering evidence and reporting the truth.

"Who do you think saved your ass back then? Who do you think negotiated that deal sending you to LA?" Cameron started walking back over to Jimmy, his hands firmly planted on his hips. "If not for me, you'd have been fish dinner."

"You'd have me believe that you destroyed my life, my career, just to save my ass?" Jimmy all but laughed out loud. "Why would you? What did you have to gain?"

"Because I took an oath to protect the people of Chicago, good or bad, and that's what I did and still do!" Cameron shook his head, looking out to the ocean and the waves lapping along the shoreline. "This time it's personal. And now I've got things of my own to take care of."

"That's a switch. It's usually 'nothing' personal with you," Jimmy accused.

"You really want to know? Dylan Cameron was my sister's son, damn it! And I promised her I'd find his killer." Cameron came so close Jimmy could feel the heat of his breath as he hissed his secret. "There's a connection with Dylan and the latest attack, and I'm going to find it. Keep an eye on Clar, Jimmy."

The words belted Jimmy in the gut. Speechless, he watched Cameron slip around the corner of the house and into the night shadows. For the first time since Chicago, Jimmy felt sympathy for the man.

CHAPTER 9

CAS Studio:
Next Day

Jimmy pushed open the door and stood back as everyone marched by. The afternoon sun filtered through the window blinds, deceptively bathing the room in warmth. Movie posters were splattered across a stark white wall behind the reception desk where the cold stare of Evie met them.

"How did I get so lucky?" Evie asked, a smirk on her plain face. "I gave you my statement already, so what do you want now?"

"Where are the cameras used on the day of the attack?" Cameron demanded leaning forward, his hands flat on the desk in front of him. The detective use of those old intimidation practices clearly weren't working at the moment. Evie Dagmyer wasn't the type of woman who wimped out when a man got in her face. She was the type who laughed loud and long.

"I don't know what you're talking about. All the equipment was put into storage after your people ransacked through everything like it was yesterday's trash, and then gave us permission to clean up the mess they left behind." Evie grinned like the Joker with an evil secret she didn't want to share. "If you want it, you'll have to contact Mr. DeLuca. He might give you permission to rummage through things, but I wouldn't bet on it. Are you a betting man, Detective Cameron?"

DeLuca? Jimmy stopped his pacing the instant his heart slammed to the pit of his stomach. *What the hell does DeLuca have to do with the studio? What's the connection between it and the Chicago crime boss? Other than Evie, that is.*

"Ah come on now, Ms. Dagmyer. We both know who runs the show around here and it isn't Mr. DeLuca, is it?" Cameron winked, the corner of his mouth curling up smugly. Thank goodness he wasn't buying Evie's coy act Jimmy saw right through. She'd honed her skills to perfection since arriving in California a few years ago.

"Mr. DeLuca has a financial interest in this company, Detective Cameron. Are you willing to upset the apple cart before it goes anywhere? Bite the hand that feeds you so to speak?" Evie batted her doe eyes to no avail. That little flirtation wasn't going to work on Cameron or any of them. Jimmy gave her an A for effort though. If she were truly the crime boss's illegitimate daughter, why would he put her in the lowly position of receptionist at an adult film studio? Maybe he doesn't know she's working here. Not a chance, DeLuca would know what his children were up to, legitimate or otherwise.

If DeLuca financially backs Cum Again Studio, then he's known where Clar's been since her parents' accident. Jimmy's blood ran ice cold with the realization. All this time he thought Clar safe from the monsters who may have killed her parents, when all along they were keeping her in their sights. Was Sal DeLuca and his family responsible for murdering Dylan Cameron as well? Cold rage went through him at the betrayal, the lack of respect. Did the mob boss's influence reach all the way to the West Coast, killing the innocent film crew and leaving Levi beaten to a pulp? If so, what did he have to gain? More so, why murder a porn star?

Damn it! Jimmy shook off the dread creeping up his spine. This was getting deeper into organized crime than any of them may have thought. As much as he hated to think of the possibility, they'd might have to bring Cameron in on their plans to go undercover, he was the expert in the crime boss area. LA couldn't be much different than Chicago where that was concerned and keeping the enemy close was the only option

"Ms. Dagmyer, we can do this the hard way and wait until I get a court order, which could uncover other unsavory items in the studio's possession. Or you can let me into that storeroom now. Unless of course you have something to hide," Cameron taunted, a menacing smirk creasing his mouth. "Do you, Ms. Dagmyer, have something to hide?"

"We all have our secrets, detective." Evie pushed away from the desk, then slid open the middle drawer. Her hand slipped inside and Cameron reached simultaneously for his shoulder harness.

"The keys, Evie, just give him the keys. We don't have time for your dramatics today." Jimmy perched on the corner of the desk, giving her his best smile. "You know me and what I've done for this company. I wouldn't do anything to harm its reputation in the business—would you?"

Evie slid her hand out, fingers linked around a set of keys. "You do like to play dirty after all, Jimmy. Now, get the hell off my desk and follow me."

——

Clar lagged behind everyone as they headed out of the reception area toward the studio. Dread slowed her step as everyone else marched down the hallway to Studio B. The knot in her stomach grew, intensifying the fear struggling to grip her soul.

Please powers that be, help me to keep it together. She prayed Evie had had enough good sense to have the studio professionally cleaned by now. Clar didn't know if she could stand the sight of blood echoing the spot where a soul became lost. Mostly she didn't know if she were brave enough to witness the blemish where Levi received his near fatal beating.

She sucked in a breath, releasing it slow and easy. *I won't let it get to me. I will get through this. I will survive. I will not cry.*

"Are you okay?" Jimmy's voice fluttered around her ear.

Clar didn't dare look at him. She'd certainly lose any semblance of control she fought to maintain, and being seen as weak didn't sit well with her. She nodded then grabbed tightly onto Jimmy's hand. It was enough of a sense of security to make the monsters reeling through her mind fade to black.

If only real life were that easy.

It had taken years for the monsters resulting from her parents' fatal car accident to disappear. Clar didn't know if she had the strength to battle them again.

"Here we are." Evie's voice crackled as she tugged open the door. The room bathed in darkness sparked to life with the flip of a switch. "Everything, except the cameras, are stored over in the storage closet at the back of the room. I don't think you'll find anything though. Your fellow experts at the precinct didn't so why should you? All the furniture and props were removed and professionally cleaned."

"Have to know what you're looking for," Cameron stated, heading over to a toppled camera. "The bozos that were here before didn't have all the information."

He bent over grabbing a leg of a fallen camera tripod, then dropped it just as quickly. "Damn, that's heavier than it looks! Why in the hell not use something more modern, like digital?"

Evie snickered loudly until Clint came up behind her. She turned, looked straight into his chest, then coughed and turned back to

Cameron struggling with the weight of the camera. Clar smiled bright inside at the sweep of agitation in Evie's eyes.

Serves her right. There's not a damn thing funny about this at all.

"Levi would only perform for reel to reel. One of his conditions." Jimmy sauntered over, grabbing one side while Cameron lifted the other. "Here, let me help with that." In a matter of moments, the discarded filming apparatus was righted as if it never left its station.

"Anyone know how to work this thing?" Cameron fingered every inch of the camera looking for something to start things rolling.

"There must be a screen somewhere." Clar walked over to the closet, every circuit of her nervous system felt on fire as she yanked open the door. *Please no hidden bloody bodies.* She scoured the items finding nothing...including film. "There's no film canisters in here. And no screen."

Jimmy flipped. "Is there any reason we can't use a wall? People use the side of the garage, we should be able to use one of the walls, right?"

"Great idea, O'Brien, if we had the film!" Cameron scowled at each of them as if they'd missed the obvious—which of course they had been putting the cart before the horse.

"I think we do." Jimmy pulled the cassettes out Clar had missed, holding them in the air. "We just need a film projector."

"I think I saw one in the closet." Clar squeaked out, trying to swallow the lump wedged in her throat.

"I can get it." Jimmy stood behind her, his body wrapped loosely around hers. Clar melted into the security, breathing deeply with relief. She nodded her head, slipping her hand from under his and watched as Jimmy retrieved the projector.

"Here we go." The projector purred to life and Jimmy flipped the light switch.

They sat in groups. Jimmy, Jacki, and Clint huddled protectively around Clar. Evie perched herself on a stool near a table, while Cameron stood within feet of her.

The film sputtered for a moment, then rolled smoothly giving away the secret it had kept hidden. They watched the horror of what happened the day blood flowed on the white enamel floor. She grabbed onto Jimmy's hand, squeezing it tightly as the images appeared on the wall.

Cameras and sound equipment sentinels in the room stood unmanned in their appointed positions. Soft music mingled with the sounds of sex throughout the set.

No one paid attention to them anymore.

Like a row of dominos one by one the film crew fell silently to the floor. No one cared they lay in their own fluids seeping onto the tiles.

Levi Andres thrust one last time then opened his eyes giving the performance of his life. He focused on his co-star. Fear swam in the blue orbs of the actress beneath him. Oh shit! He froze then flew into the air. His shoulder jammed onto the floor hard landing between two cameras, knocking one over.

Levi scooted deep into a dark corner away from the gurgling cries of his co-star echoing through the room. Bloody hands covered his ears as he detached himself from reality. Clar knew he was going to the safe place in his head.

Death had entered the room like a demon in the night.

A large dark mass hovered over him like a junkyard dog ready to pounce on a piece of meat. Levi curled into a fetal position as a boot made contact with his ribs and abdomen. His screams bounced around the soundproof studio as repeated kicks hit his body one right after the other.

Weak and on his knees, they heard the crack of his jaw as the pain of repeated blows seared on. Clar sucked in a sob, but couldn't shake the fear icing over her heart. Why was this happening? Who would want to harm him or his movie family? They were all dead—everyone in the studio had died, and for what?

The blows kept coming, one right after another. Then it was over and Levi's face said it all—he thought he would die. Blood trickled onto his lips, and he dropped to the floor like a bag of dirty laundry. The last thing they all heard as he fell into unconsciousness ...

"I'll have a bag of candy kisses, please."

Large pink candy wrappers from a pink striped box with KK printed across it fluttered to the floor, and the screen went black.

"I haven't used those boxes in months!" Clar quivered inside like a hummingbird gathering nectar, only the sweet taste was bitter. The tears fell and she kept swiping them away. "I changed my packaging once I decided to open the store inventory to mail order. There was a limited number of those pink boxes and wrappers."

"Then how could a person get one without..." Jimmy whispered.

Clar sunk to the floor, one hand on her chest. Tears streamed freely down flushed cheeks to the corner of her mouth. "They would have had to come into the store."

CHAPTER 10

"Where were you when the attack happened, Ms. Dagmyer?" Cameron loomed over Evie; his face crinkled in deep thought.

Evie sat in silence; her face free of any emotion other than a hint of a smirk at the corner of her mouth. "Well, I believe I was in the back office doing my job, Detective. Can I give you any witnesses to that fact? No, all but one is dead and he's not really talking much these days, is he?"

Evie's response about the victims burned like acid in the bottom of Clar's stomach. Surely Evie wouldn't have anything to do with the murders. She'd been sobbing her ass off on the phone, unless it was all an act to get attention. True, Levi had spurred the plain looking Evie's advances as gently as possible. He'd politely declined, revealing women weren't listed on his hook-up menu choices. Evie didn't have a lot of friends. Even so, Cameron had to be barking up the wrong tree if he considered the socially inept Evie a suspect.

"Detective Cameron, you can't for one moment think Evie had anything to do with this." Clar spat, taking a protective stand near the woman who'd always driven her crazy. Evie Dagmyer may not be the prettiest egg in the Easter Basket and she may come off as the last person you'd want for a friend, but she was probably the smartest chick Clar had ever met.

Clar didn't like the way Evie treated people, mostly women, especially those who were considered beautiful. But murder out of jealousy or for revenge? No, Clar didn't believe that for a minute.

Cameron spun on his heel, his black gaze raking Clar from head to toe. "Ms. Turner, if you don't mind, I'll conduct my investigation as I see fit. It might do you good to remember that you are all here at my pleasure. If you don't pipe down, I will take Ms. Dagmyer down to head-quarters, place her under arrest as a suspect, and continue my questioning in an interrogation room."

"Let the man do his job." Jacki's voice washed over Clar, soothing the fire burning through her with the coolness of her tone. "Cameron's taking a chance with his own career by allowing us here. He's a bit unorthodox if not unethical, we still need to find out anything possible to ferret out a lead."

Clar nodded, then reluctantly sunk into a chair on the other side of the room, away from the interrogation. She needed to get a grip in order to think. She mentally started to go through the hundreds of faces that had come into her store the six months she'd been open on weekends only. That was the only time she'd been using those damn cotton candy pink boxes for in-store orders only. Cutting more corners, she'd taken to personally scrolling double Ks across each box and wrapper until she could afford the more expensive personalized pink and black striped linen boxes.

No matter how hard she tried, the only face she visualized was Levi's, bloodied and bruised. Pretty wrapped candy boxes couldn't chase it away.

"I can't just sit here, Jacki. There's someone out there using my candy business as a vessel for their sick crime. I've got to find out who in the hell it is and why my candy of all things." Clar jumped out of the worn cloth chair, her insides twisted like a pretzel. She had to get out of there, away from the movie posters and a life she'd left behind.

"You mean 'we,' don't you, Clar." Jimmy pulled her into his arms, and she immediately melted into his warmth and security. "We'll figure this out together."

"Jimmy, what am I going to do? Do we go with the plan Jacki and Clint came up with?" Glancing over at the detective and Evie, Clar believed they really had no choice. Trusting Cameron to handle things would take too long. In her heart Clar was scared they didn't have that luxury to allow the scales of the law to balance things out. There was a killer on the loose and Clar intended to stop him, even if it meant using herself as a pawn in the killing spree.

There, I've made up my mind. A sense of relief and determination washed over her. Like her father, she would sacrifice herself for another human being. Once a cop's daughter, always a cop's daughter.

"First, we need to wait and find out what Cameron comes up with. All we can do is sit back and let him do his job, and listen. Maybe something will spark your memory." Jimmy suggested in a hushed voice.

"Yeah, like the face of a murderer in my store buying my candy!" Clar snapped then slipped away from Jimmy. She stormed out the door far from the continuous badgering Cameron instilled onto Evie.

———ℓ———

"Listen, Detective, other than the crew and actors the only other person who came into the office that day was Eddie DeLuca." Evie fiddled with the hem of her shirt. She sighed inwardly; *I just wish everyone would go away. If he's going to arrest me let him, Eddie won't let me sit behind bars for long. Daddy would kill him if he did.*

Cameron looked up from his note taking, eyebrows raised in surprise. "How long has Edward DeLuca been in town?"

Evie smiled like the Cheshire Cat. "You didn't know he was here? I'm surprised Daddy Dearest didn't tell you he'd sent his 'legitimate' son to look after his 'illegitimate' sister."

"What surprises me is that he'd do it at all if Sal wasn't concerned about you, Evie. Just what have you been up to since coming out here?" Cameron pulled a chair across the room, the legs scraping the white tiled floor like chalk across a chalkboard. "What has your twin brother been doing?"

"I wish I could answer that for you." Evie smirked. "All I know is one day I got in the elevator and there he was like we'd always been loving siblings. For whatever reason, he'd decided to move to LA, purchase the condo above me, and move right into my life. Like I needed him. What a jerk. He can go back to Chicago for all I care." *Had she said too much? If Cameron didn't know Eddie was in town does that mean he no longer works for Sal? No, Daddy would have told her. Wouldn't he have?* "As for me, I wished he'd go back to Chicago and let me handle my life as I see fit. I like running the studio, being the boss suits me. Eddie is the thorn in my side I can't pull out since the day he followed me into the world."

"No love lost then." Cameron scribbled across his notebook, pausing momentarily before flipping it closed. "Let's talk about Levi Andres."

"What's there to talk about? He's a porn star who prefers men to women...on and off the screen." A twinge of hatred spun through Evie. At one time she'd vowed to make Levi pay for that rejection of her. Now he lay in a hospital bed. It looked like fate was on her side for once in her life.

"What about his relationship with Clar Turner?" Cameron's eyes glistened with curiosity.

"Professionally or personally?" Evie drummed her fingers on the table. Tap. Tap. Tap tap tap. Tap. Tap. Tap tap tap.

"Both. Were there any times that they may have disagreed on a film?" Cameron flattened his hand over hers, halting the cadence.

"Cameron, you're digging a hole you won't be able to get out of with that line of questioning!" Jimmy hissed, his back rigid.

Evie stifled a response and smiled, knowing full well that two bulls were about to lock horns and she didn't want to miss it. To her disappointment, the two stared each other down instead, each waiting for the other to make the first move.

"Oh hell, why don't the two of you just get on with it and finish what you started in Chicago? After all, isn't that what you both want? To beat each other senseless until neither of you can stand?" They both stiffened at her words. *Score!* Evie laughed, accomplishment soaring through her. She'd made her point and touched the sore spot each of them carried. *This is going to be good!*

Cameron stood, casting his shadow over her like a black menacing mass she'd never be able to shake. "If you are done, Ms. Dagmyer, answer my question."

"I'll tell you what I know." Evie swallowed hard, her gaze traveling over everyone in the room...everyone except Clar.

Jimmy stood near the door keeping an eye on the hall. Somewhere down in the abyss the woman he loved tore herself apart with blame. He knew Clar well enough to know she'd not rest until all her questions were answered. To discover why she'd become a lunatic's target.

"Cameron, whatever you need to know I'll tell you." Jimmy dangled a carrot, hoping to snare a jackass.

Jacki came up next to him, placing a hand on his arm. "Jimmy, don't open that can of worms."

"She's not here to do it, so I have to." Jimmy smiled, then pulled up a chair across the table from Cameron and Evie. Jacki and Clint gathered round the end, for support and to fill in any blanks. "I hope you have plenty of paper, Detective."

Cameron nodded, flipping the page. "How do you know Levi Andres?"

"After leaving Chicago under, shall we say, less than desirable conditions I lived on the beach until my bank book was emptied. Knowing I needed to find work, a surfing buddy told me about an opening at SXY. I contacted them, interviewed, and got the job. They didn't give a rat's ass about the Chicago trouble; they were impressed with my credentials. My first assignment was covering a debut film. Little did I know I'd be covering a gay man playing it straight pretending to have sex with women. Levi became Cum Again Studio's biggest grossing male star."

"What about Clar, how does she fit into the picture?" Cameron ceased his chicken scratching and flipped to a clean page.

"As you know, Clar's parents were killed in a car accident after her father retired from the police force. They were on their way to see her in college, but never made it." Jimmy leaned in toward Cameron, locking his gaze onto the detective's. "You also know her father was Karl Turner."

Cameron's pen halted abruptly. "Yes, I know."

"Yes, the same. One of the few honest cops in Chicago who wouldn't bend to the mob. Who had a list a mile long of everyone who was ever on DeLuca's payroll...including you." Jimmy watched the detective squirm slightly then grasp for a small thread of integrity.

"A long time ago. Please continue."

"Clar was devastated and fell off the deep end. She quit school, and pretty much took up to living on the beach. She and Levi became friends, and he introduced her to a way of escaping the reality of her parents' deaths.

She changed her appearance, complete with breast implants and bleach blonde hair. Kandi Kyses was born and took the adult film industry by storm. It wasn't long before she became a very well-off woman with a past she'd tried to forget—and she did for a long time. I covered everything about her. When I realized she was hiding from something, I did some digging. That's when I found her connection to Karl Turner."

"And that's where I came into the picture," Jacki interjected, moving into a vacant spot next to Jimmy. "Clar walked into my office one day looking to hire me. She wanted to find out more about her parents' accident. After months of digging, I came up with nothing. It was an accident, plain and simple."

"Ms. Wolfe, nothing is plain and simple. And 'accidents' can stay just that for eternity." Cameron shook his head, a look of remorse in his eyes.

Damn, the man does have a conscience after all.

"But there's more to it, isn't there?" Clint interjected, hovering at the end of the table near Evie.

"As far as Clar was concerned, she felt the way to honor her parents' memories was to take a step into their lives. She enrolled in classes for baking and candy making which were her mother's favorite past-times. She talked to me about classes on becoming a private investigator, and enrolled into classes at the area tech school. She eventually became one of my students, and one of my closest and trusted friends. I'd go to the ropes for her."

She never found out how the accident happened?" Cameron asked.

Jimmy stared across the table; his hidden hands clutched in tight fists. "No, but we both know how that can be rectified, don't we?"

CHAPTER 11

24 Hours
Later

"The adult film industry was recently rocked with the brutal murders of members of the film crew in addition to the attempted murder of Cum Again Studio's top male star, Levi Andres. It is reported that the near death of Andres has prompted the return of Kandi Kyses. As soon as we can get an interview with CAS representatives, we'll bring you up to date. Reporting from Cum Again Studios, this is James O'Brien for SXY."

Hands trembling, Clar turned off the TV. She dreaded what the next few minutes would bring. Outside, in front of cameras, she'd have to re-invent Kandi Kyses. She'd have to give a performance convincing enough to lure a killer out from hiding. The same crazed maniac that probably killed Dylan last year. The nutcracker who murdered the studio film crew. The killer who'd left Levi near dead with a message just for her.

What had any of them done to that person? What had she done to provoke these murders?

Clar drew in a deep breath then adjusted the skullcap, hardly recognizing the image staring back at her. The tight, diving V neck top barely concealed the fleshy breastplate. Her full figure pinched from being squeezed into a waist-cinching garment that she'd sworn off a year ago. The makeup made her feel more like a clown than a beautiful woman. The person she'd vowed to never be again emerged slowly from the depths leaving a sour taste in her mouth.

"I don't know if I can pull this off, Jacki. I worked hard to have a normal life." Clar fought the urge to let the tears stinging her eyes stream down. "It's been a while since I've acted.

I buried the person I was back then over a year ago. And now..."

"I know. If it's too much, then don't do this. We'll think of a different way to get the guy." Jacki stood nearby in the shadows. She'd become one of Clar's pillars of support on this scheme of theirs to catch the murderer. "And for the record. You haven't changed, only the packaging is different."

"Going undercover isn't the issue, I'm at peace with that." Clar grabbed the long blonde Farrah Fawcett 70's style wig, stroking its golden fibers while her stomach twisted in knots. "I never in a million years thought I'd be back here."

"Hey, look at it this way. The Elvira breastplate saved you from getting implants again."

"Geez, leave it to you to come up with that!" Clar laughed, the tension of doubt ebbing. "I signed up to do this and I'll go through with it. Just hope it works the way we planned it."

"Don't worry. Clint will be in the studio with you and I'll be out front with Evie screening everyone who comes in and out. Jimmy is on the street with his ear to the ground. If something's amiss, we'll know about it." Jacki's reflection stepped into the mirror, frustration creasing her otherwise beautiful face. "We've got your back."

The clean faced, beautiful cowgirl Clar knew and loved had been replaced by a modern-day

Jezebel. Complete with exposed breasts peeking out of her top, big hair the color of the setting sun on a winter's day, and more makeup on her face than any cosmetic company had in product.

Clar turned, stifling a giggle. "You, um, well..."

"Look like I belong in a porn movie?" Jacki quipped, tucking her bulging breasts back into the bra. "No disrespect intended."

"Let's just say your assets will draw some attention." Clar chuckled. "Clint will have a...hard ...time of it for sure."

"Exactly what I was afraid of." Jacki tugged at the hairpiece. "The last thing I need is that ex-Ranger on my trail."

"Um, I think he's exactly what you need. A warm body on those icy winter nights. Picture him putting up hay or working Max. Yum is what comes to mind." Clar winked, then turned back to her own reflection.

For a moment she'd forgotten about their plan. She'd forgotten she'd be going back in front of the camera, real or not. She'd forgotten a murderer was out there hunting for her, if the wrappers scattered on the floor around Levi meant anything. And the cryptic message about wanting more candy kisses. What else could it mean other than someone was out to get her?

Standing, Clar shook out her arms and hands. Sucking in a deep breath, she scrutinized the reflection looking back at her. *As good as it's going to get. Ready. Set. Shoot.* With a curt nod Clar said, "Let's see if Clint is ready and get this shindig started."

———·❧·———

Clar walked into the front office, her hips and breasts swaying with each step as she inched her way toward Jimmy. Every blood cell in his body went into a turbo boil of lust. Exit Clar Turner. Enter Kandi Kyses.

A low whistle floated around the room. "Wow! What the hell happened to Clar? Where is she?" Clint mocked concern looking around the room before sliding up next to Jimmy. "Damn! You are one hell of a lucky man, O'Brien."

Jimmy had all but forgotten what this side of Clar looked like. Yes, she was sexually slutty as hell and looked ready for action. Yes, his damn penis reacted like any normal male would making his pants a bit uncomfortable. Did she really turn him on heart and soul? Not as Kandi Kyses, adult film star. It was Clar Turner, candy maker, who pushed his buttons. Underneath all the goop and costume was the woman he adored.

"Looks like I'm not the only one," Jimmy remarked as Jacki followed Clar into the office.

"Hmph, I prefer my women with horse shit on their boots, not their face." Clint smiled, picked up the camera sitting on the desk, turned and adjusted the crotch of his pants.

Jimmy chuckled, shaking his head in amusement. "And you accused me of having it bad."

Both Clar and Jacki scowled, tossed their heads, then flipped a shoulder at them. Jimmy burst out loud with laughter. "I guess we've been flipped off, Mason."

Jimmy glanced at his watch. Two o'clock and no sight of Evie. "Has anyone heard from our favorite receptionist today?" Thumbing through an appointment book on her desk, he noted she'd penciled in today's interview. He knew she'd at least would have known they were going to be there today. What the hell could be keeping her?

Clar turned, her face scrunched with worry. "No, it's not like her. But then again, this is all about me and Levi, so who knows. Maybe she's caught up in traffic. Or wants to make a grand entrance."

"Maybe." Something unsettling prickled at the back of Jimmy's neck. "If we don't hear from her by the time we're done, then I'm calling Cameron. We can't delay this any longer though. Jacki, can you manage until she shows up?"

"I think I can handle what walks through that door," Jacki said, pulling up to the desk. "While I'm here I'll do a little digging of my own."

"Clar—ur Kandi—your adoring public awaits your arrival," Jimmy said, lightly squeezing her hand. Gawd, how he wanted so much more from her. This wasn't the time, but it would be and the sooner the better. Or he'd have to find a way to relieve the pressure mounting between his thighs. "Give me a few minutes to set up and then make your entrance.

"Clint, stay close in case the killer is hanging around. The last thing I want to report on is the live assassination of Kandi Kyses."

"You got it." Clint swung the camera on his shoulder and pushed through the door to the parking lot.

"Jacki, are you sure you're okay in here alone?" Clar looked at her friend, worry etched across her face.

"Yes, now get the heck out of here. We can't catch a fly without the honey." Jacki waved them away from the desk and the task she'd set out to do.

Jimmy took Clar's elbow and leaned in, "Don't worry, I'd never let anything happen to you." He followed Clint's path, dread squeezing around his heart.

I hope we're doing the right thing here. Damn, I should have told Cameron!

Clar stood peering out the door's smoky tinted window. Every fear she'd had was pushed aside into a part of her mind no one would be able to reach. The person she'd worked hard to become neatly packed away for safe keeping. She could do this. She had to do this.

"Clar, I'll be standing just outside at the end of the walk, waiting for you." Jimmy pointed out the window toward the sign that marked the studio's entrance. "Clint, I'll need you to be in a position that will keep me on camera but also give you the ability to stay aware of the surroundings."

"How will I know when you want me to come out?" Clar hoped to delay Jimmy from leaving her alone with her thoughts. What was she worried about? Some newscast about her return? Questions about where she's been? How she felt about the recent murders and Levi's near-death beating? Hell yeah, every one of them.

"Don't worry, I'll handle the story until you're ready. Remember to just go with whatever I come up with regarding the attack." Jimmy placed a reassuring hand on her arm and gave it a light squeeze. "I have to ask, Clar, you know that."

Clar rubbed the tingle of fire that spread under her skin straight to the tips of her painted toes. "Of course you do, it's your job. It's what you're good at. Just don't fawn all over me like you used to. That's all I ask."

"If I don't people will wonder what's up." Jimmy brushed his lips at the corner of her mouth, blazing her with desire. "It'll be like not riding a bike for a while for a few minutes, but then you'll remember right away once things get rolling."

Jimmy pushed through the doors to the outside, Clint a few steps behind, camera slung onto his shoulder.

"That's what I'm worried about—remembering." Glancing at the wall clock, Clar drew in a shaky breath. She'd give him a few minutes to get the broadcast set then go out to her adoring public. Adoring indeed. Somewhere out there was a killer who wanted her and she didn't think it was for pleasure.

She was still trying to process everything. All the images of recent customers hadn't sparked a warning bell, neither did any of the on-line orders. Whoever it was had to have been in her shop, but when? What the hell had she done to provoke such horrible actions?

"Clar, would you turn on the TV so I can help keep an eye on things out there? Clint might miss something." Jacki never peeked over the top of the monitor on Evie's desk. She'd been working on breaking the password code so that she'd have access to any records.

Evie hadn't shown up for work yet, that in itself was unusual. She was as punctual as the church bells announcing the hour. Clar wondered what kind of game Evie was up to and why.

Clar pressed the on button. "You've got your head buried already. How do you plan to do both? Break the code and watch the broadcast?"

"As soon as I hear O'Brien's voice it'll have my devoted attention." Jacki continued to peck away at the keyboard, writing down word sequences as she went along. It was going to be a long process, but if anyone could find out what Evie's password was, it would be Jackson Wolfe.

"We interrupt this program for breaking news. We have James O'Brien at Cum Again Studios where it is rumored the queen of adult films, Kandi Kyses, is on the premises. James, what do you have for us so far?"

"Thank you, Charles. I can tell you the rumor is no longer a rumor. Kandi Kyses did indeed return sometime late last night in a black truck. Why she's here and where she's been is a matter of speculation. One can only imagine it's been the latest attacks that has brought her back to the studio. As soon as there is more developing news, I'll let you know. Thank you, Charles. For SXY, this is James O'Brien."

"There you have it, folks, the buxom blonde has indeed returned to Cum Again Studios. As soon as we have any new developments, we'll bring you up to date."

CHAPTER 12

Damn! They've already started. Screw it. That fucking LA traffic on the 101 blew my plan out of the water or I would have been in place before it all started. Now I've got to find a way to get into position without being detected. Tough, but not impossible with these morons, they are so predictable.

"This is James O'Brien for SXY coming to you live with an update from outside Cum Again Studios where Kandi Kyses is inside. Kandi Kyses has agreed to a brief interview. We are expecting her at any moment. Could she be returning to the screen? Or is she here to be at the bedside of fellow star, Levi Andres. As you all know, Mr. Andres was brutally attacked and left to die alongside one of his co-stars and the entire film crew. The police still have no suspects and no leads in this case, nor the Dylan Cameron cold case.

"Kandi Kyses quietly left the studio a year ago without a trace. The question burning on everyone's mind is why? Why leave at the height of her film career? Where did she go when she retired? What was she doing? At one time, this reporter heard something about chocolate and bunnies. That lead left me with chocolate on my face and licking my chops.

"Looks like Ms. Kyses is on her way." The camera swung, capturing Kandi Kyses as she sashayed through the door and down the walk, head held high, hips swaying with each step. Long blonde hair waved through the California breeze, free and easy.

"Kandi Kyses, let me say on behalf of every red-blooded man out there—thank you for coming back. We've all missed you. I've missed following your outstanding career."

"Thank you, James. I missed all of you too." Kandi smiled, the tip of her tongue lingering for a brief moment on her upper ruby red lip.

"Careful now, you'll make me blush and ruin my tough guy image. Let's put all the innuendos aside and get to the heart of the matter. Your fans and admirers want to know where you've been for the past year. I couldn't even get a bead on you, and believe me, I've tried."

"Now, Jimmy." Kandi sucked in her bottom lip, running a fingertip over Jimmy's mouth. "A girl's gotta have some secrets, doesn't she? I've been preparing for my next roll and film, that's all. It takes time, my love."

"Yes, I guess it does, but just the same I have so many questions to ask you. Where have you been? Up until lately it's been pretty boring around here without you. Does your retirement have something to do with chocolate and bunnies? Or are you here to comfort Levi Andres? What's the real reason for your return?"

"My, aren't you full of questions? Some of which have no validation to even entertain answering, I'm sure." Kandi flipped her blonde hair at the camera, then winked. "As you know, Levi is a good friend of mine. Off screen, he's been like a little brother to me. When I heard he'd had an accident, I knew I had to be at his side. Family takes care of family, that's what I've always believed."

"Yes, but how do you feel about what has happened? First the murder of Dylan Cameron on set with the killer yet to be found, followed by your sudden retirement. Now the deaths, and the brutal beating of Levi while on set in the middle of a scene, about to make love to his co-star. Some may say you know more than anyone and that you're afraid to come forward. Do you believe these two incidents are inter-connected? Do you think it's the same killer? Or just a copycat. What makes you think you being here is going to help solve a cold case and the recent homicides?"

SMACK! Kandi's hand splattered across the reporter's face, sending a message loud and clear.

"Mr. O'Brien, I believe this interview is over!" The camera followed Kandi as she stomped her way back into the studio, shaking her hand.

Hmph. Andres is no more a movie star than my big toe. More like odd man out with the ladies. As I thought, Andres's beating had been too good for her to resist not coming back to LA. Ha, mission accomplished!

I can see why every man in the world lusts after her. Kandi Kyses movies are highly sought after because of what she does to a man. Hell, I've got a boner just watching her strut. Granted, she's not the thinner woman of a year ago. Her body's fuller with sexy womanly curves begging to be manipulated. Yeah, well, looks are deceiving. Never trust a woman who makes chocolate like she's having pretend sex. Rich. Delicious. Mouth-watering.

She smiled at O'Brien like he was a popsicle for her to lick slow and easy. She makes me sick. What kind of black magic does she use to get every man wanting her? I'll find out her secret and use it to my advantage, then destroy her. I'll take back what should rightfully be mine from birth.

Sickening, totally sickening. So full of shit! She's no more returning to what they call acting than I am. Maybe if they knew how big of a liar she is, they'd cast her aside like yesterday's garbage. Her deception runs deep and dark as a black hole. Time to bring it to light. To expose her. To have her pay for the sins against others. Against family. Against me.

There we go, let's get to the real reason why the bitch is back, O'Brien. Tell them who brought you back, bitch!

The look on her face couldn't have been more precious. She was pissed! Her pursed mouth made her head look like it could explode with nails driving right into O'Brien's face. Ha, that would have been great! I'd have him out of the way and no one would be none the wiser.

Shit, that left hook had to hurt! Left the bastard with his big mouth hung to the floor. I'll reward her for it. Then I'll take my revenge like I did with the others.

Kandi will wish she never returned and had stayed up north with her chocolate bunnies. But I need her here to complete what I've started with

Dylan Cameron. I want what's mine and I'm going to get it!

As for the cops, they'll be chasing their tails for a long time before they find me. And by the time they do, Kandi Kyses will be anything but kissable.

⎯⎯⎯ 𝓮𝓮𝓮 ⎯⎯⎯

"What the hell was that all about out there? Are you pissed because I didn't fawn all over you?" Jimmy rubbed the red mark fanned across his cheek, the shock of it lingered in his eyes.

Clar hoped it stung as much as her hand. It took all she had to keep from shaking the sting away, instead she massaged the center of her palm with the pad of her thumb.

"No, you asshole! Drilling me about Dylan, and then Levi. And that shit about where I've been?" Clar backed up, waving everyone from her. "What the hell was I supposed to say? You made me feel like a complete piece of mindless fluff."

She didn't want to calm down. She didn't want anyone telling her to calm down. She had the right to be pissed off. But at who and what expense? To make their act as convincing as possible in case the killer was watching? Even now, away from the camera, she wanted to keep acting this out, not to let her guard down. She didn't want anyone else to get killed if she eased up for a second. That scared the hell out of her more than her portrayal during the interview.

Clar swallowed an acid lump of regret lodged in her throat. With so much at stake, she wouldn't back down regardless of how much she wanted to. Everything had to go according to plan, even if feelings got hurt along the way. Improvise Jimmy had said. He didn't say anything about hearts breaking. Or losing the trust she'd started to feel for him.

"That, out there, was not what I agreed to. Not one damn bit. You haven't changed, James O'Brien. Always after a story no matter the cost. Trying to make an innocent person out to be a guilty shit head. Don't *ever* come near me again!" Clar reached out to steady herself. The room spun slowly, causing her to take a few deep breaths. If she didn't calm down, she'd be sucked into a drain of swirling shit.

Breathe, slow and easy. 1. 2. 3. Breathe in, blow out.

"Do you have something to be guilty of, Ms. Turner? Is there some information you're hiding that could shed light on the recent attacks?" Jimmy popped the wall with his hand, his back ramrod straight with anger and frustration. "Damn it! What the hell do you want from me, Clar? I've given you everything—"

"Congratulations, you've reminded me why I tried to avoid you as much as possible for years. All you've given me is pain in my ass. Just get the hell out of my life, O'Brien! I never want to see you again." Clar grit her teeth, giving Jimmy a shove in the chest. Him grilling her hadn't been part of the plan as she knew it. That's the press for you, give them an inch and they take it all the way to the twilight zone. "You broke your promise to me about doing this interview!"

"Promise? I didn't promise you a damn thing. I told you I may ask about Levi and where you disappeared to." Jimmy rubbed the back of his neck, confusion burning in his eyes. "What the hell did you expect, that we'd sit down for tea and biscuits and have a leisurely chat about the weather or the current fashion trend? I did this because you fucking forced me to against my better judgement, and then you flip out on me."

"How dare you make light of my feelings!" Clar glared at Jimmy, shaking, unable to control her emotions. She thought she'd been prepared, but she was wrong. He'd turned back into Jimmy the newshound before her eyes and she'd freaked. Hell, she was still freaking. She couldn't help overreacting. The interview didn't go as she'd expected. She'd no idea that he'd be such an ass and make her out to be a wanna be savior. "You insinuated I thought I was back to save the day. We both know that's as far from the truth as possible."

Maybe I'm not cut out to do this undercover stuff after all. Why did I think I could be like dad? What made me think James O'Brien and I could work together, finally after all these years? When this is done and the killer's behind bars, I'm going to pack up Levi, head home, and try to salvage what's left of my new life.

"Can you two hold it down?" Clint stepped between them, pushing Jimmy back a step or two by thumping him in the chest. "You, my friend, are acting like a damn jerk!"

"Hell, if I am! Miss High-And-Mighty started this." Jimmy snatched his backpack, shoving the station mic into it. Next, the camera jostled into its case, the lid snapping shut. "She's mad, totally mad." Jimmy shoved past Clint then grazed the man coming through the door without a second glance back at Clar. "You all can deal with her, I'm done."

The urge to break down and cry raged in Clar. What the hell had she done?

⸻ℓℓℓ⸻

After the night on the beach, sweet feelings started to emerge. All hope of her heart's true desire gone in minutes because she couldn't handle the press. Hell, the press couldn't handle her. The press being James O'Brien!

A sour reminder of why she refused to have a relationship. No one wanted a broken woman who hid her true self by having sex in front of a camera to escape reality, even if it was all fake. Someone like James O'Brien was totally out of her realm of possibilities. Clar couldn't wait to get back to Wisconsin and try to find that peaceful life she'd had a few days ago.

She swiped at a tear, her gaze settling on the man who came in as Jimmy was going out. He waved, a sly smile of amusement across his face. "Hi, how's everyone doing?"

He reminded Clar of someone, but she couldn't pinpoint who. Probably one of those people who had a common face and looked like everyone. Still the back of her neck prickled a warning.

"Who the hell are you?" Clint placed himself firmly between the stranger, Jacki and Clar. She didn't think the guy was a threat even though Ranger Mason appeared out of the blue.

"Me? I'm Edward DeLuca, I'm here to see Evie Dagmyer."

Evie...his smile reminds me of Evie! Great, and I had to throw a tizzy and chase away Jimmy.

"Evie? She hasn't come in yet today." Clar looked Eddie over head to toe. Dressed in a black suit, blue shirt, and striped tie, he was neat as a button. The exact opposite of Evie, who always appeared as if she'd thrown something on from the clothes hamper.

"Did you say your name was DeLuca? As in the Chicago DeLuca family?" Jacki asked, looking up from the computer screen she'd been intensely studying. Her gazed traveled over Eddie pausing briefly at every possible spot where a gun could be hidden.

"One and the same. Why, is that a problem?" Eddie smiled, shoving his hands into his pockets then leaned onto the wall. He locked his gaze onto Clar.

"I'm a little curious as to why someone from a Chicago crime family would be looking for Evie Dagmyer," Clint stated as casual as a defender of the public could. Even with Jacki sitting behind the reception desk, Clar felt more at ease with the tough cowboy figure Clint represented. Jacki was fierce and could take care of herself, but Clint was the trained professional—Texas Ranger style.

"It's not so strange a brother looking for his sister, now, is it?" Eddie pushed from the wall; his gaze locked on Clint. "The old mob ways have been gone for a while. Or haven't you heard Sal DeLuca has turned over a new leaf. The old man has gone legit."

"Evie hadn't said anything about expecting a brother today. In fact, she rarely ever mentions family." Clar's eyes bore into Eddie even as she flipped through the appointment book on Evie's desk. Why wouldn't Evie say her brother was coming in today? "Nothing is noted on her calendar and she's a stickler for writing appointments down. And since you're here looking for her, that tells me you haven't heard from her either. She never called to say she wasn't going to be here today, and if I know Evie as well as I think I do, she isn't one to miss a day of work. Even if she's on her deathbed."

"In all fairness to Evie, she didn't know I was going to be in town." Eddie moved with the ease of a panther. Graceful and with purpose, gliding across the floor. "We haven't spoken recently. It's been a number of years since we've seen each other. We have the usual sibling feelings for each other, more times than not we agree to disagree. Our family is, how shall I put it? Competitive in nature, if you know what I mean, as well as unpredictable."

"I'm well aware of the competitiveness within the DeLuca Family—blood or not. Your father's infamous even in Texas." Clint's voice carried a bag full of suspicion.

"Mr. DeLuca, it's nice to finally meet a member of Evie's family. She rarely, if ever, speaks of them." Clar rose, extending her hand out to Eddie. "As soon as I hear from Evie, I'll be sure to tell her you stopped by."

"Thank you, Miss?" Eddie clasped both hands around hers, his touch as light as a wispy cloud.

"Kandi, Kandi Kyses." Clar didn't see any reason to break character with this man. There was no real proof that Eddie DeLuca really was Evie's brother or not.

"Miss Kyses, it's a fantasy come true meeting you in person. Evie will definitely be surprised, and disappointed she missed me—at least I hope she is. It was great meeting everyone. Have a great day." Eddie smiled, gave her hand a light kiss, then headed toward the door.

Eddie's movie star looks should have landed him on the big screen, and his coffee brown eyes drew her in. Everything about him made her uneasy and on guard. The term *slick rick* charged through her mind in a flashing blaze of red. Wiping her hand free of the kiss, she gazed out the door gathering her wits about her. There was something very unsettling about him.

Okay, so he's Evie's brother. That doesn't mean he's anything like her and you know it. You're still pissed at Jimmy and taking it out on this poor guy.

"Jacki, did you record the broadcast?" Clint asked, pulling out a chair that Clar plopped into.

The perfect place for her to sulk and have a pity party of one. Damn it! She'd come too far to accept that invite again. One party like that in a lifetime is more than enough, even for her.

"What do you think, cowboy?" Jacki spat, coming to Clar's side. "Are you okay?"

"Oh, I don't know, what do you think? I slapped a member of the press across the face. Most likely will get carted away by Cameron, charged with assault, and spend the rest of my life behind bars. Levi lays in a hospital bed unable to put two coherent words together. My candy business is suffering because I'm here chasing a killer. I've probably lost my only chance at happiness. And then to find out that Evie has a brother who seems to be the polar opposite of her, yet not. Other than that, I'm peachy." Clar laughed nervously, knowing full well this was the tip of the iceberg. She wished Jimmy were there instead of having stomped off like a little boy who'd gotten his hands slapped for snatching a cookie out of the jar.

"Let's settle down and take a look at the recording. I didn't see anything suspicious, but that doesn't mean someone wasn't lurking out there." Clint grabbed the DVR and headed down the hall toward Studio A, where the latest murders had taken place.

"What about Jimmy? Shouldn't he be here as well?" Clar pushed out of the chair and her world snatched her back to reality. She'd have rather stayed in the world of make believe behind the camera where she knew what the next line would be. "He has a keen eye for this investigative stuff."

Jacki looked up from gathering the sheets of information she'd garnered from Evie's computer. "Technically he should be, but he's not. It was his choice to walk out."

"Yes, but I can't help but feel that I drove him to it. That I'd taken things a bit too far."

"He'll get over it, now let's get started," Clint called back from the hallway seconds before pulling open the studio door. "I'll get things set up."

"Clar?"

"Yeah?" Clar turned, feeling Jacki's hand around her arm.

"He'll be back," Jacki said, then swept past her and into Studio A.

If only Clar could be so sure, she might feel better. If wishes truly did come true, he would ride up on his white steed and continue searching for the killer with them. Knights riding white horses up to the castle to save the damsel only appeared in fairy tales, and Clar's life had been as far from a fairy tale as one could get.

"I figured if we each take a third of the screen, the chances of us missing anything is low." Clint stood at a table in the back of the room, the DVR hooked up to the home theater projector.

Jacki sat in the middle of the room, shuffling her notes on the table. Clar knew from experience Jacki would have everything sorted in date order for easy viewing. Clar pulled a chair to the far left where she'd be able to concentrate on her third of the screen.

"Well, I guess I can get rid of this now." Clar slid the long blonde wig from her head, followed by the skull cap. She ran a hand through her now flattened spiked cinnamon colored hair. It felt like a cool breeze had come into the room relieving the heat that had been trapped there. "I hate these damn things. I never want to wear one again. It's amazing how one gets used to less hair; feels great in the heat of summer."

"I'll settle for a ponytail," Jacki said, pulling her hair up from her neck.

"I hope so, I don't know many cowgirls with short hair," Clint said, flipping the lights off. "I prefer women with a long flowing mane, which is why I own mares instead of studs. I also like them sweet smelling, not like the overuse of perfume someone in this room has on."

"Are you sure it's not your overuse of after-shave, Clint? It's overwhelming in this room," Jacki shot back.

"Can you two knock it off, and just start the damn DVR?" Clar chided, hoping sooner or later they would get together to settle the dust stirred up between them.

The interview finally started to replay on the wall across from the projector. Clar smiled seeing Jimmy doing what he loved, report the news even if it was staged this time around. Damn the man was sexy as hell, more now than when she'd first met him on the beach. That was a lifetime ago, long before her film career when they were both wandering aimlessly through life.

"I'm going to start again and slow it down as much as I can. Make sure you're not watching the interview, you both need to keep your eye on the background," Clint said as the projector came to life again, exposing even the smallest movement they'd all made.

Clar cringed when she saw her hand land on Jimmy's cheek. Her heart bled with grief. Pulling her gaze from the two of them, she concentrated on the edge of the building catching a shadow in the hedges. "Clint, can you back that up?"

"Yeah, how far?"

"A few seconds. I thought I saw movement, but it could be nothing." Clar stood closer to the wall, her vision concentrating on the thick hedges lining the corner of the studio. "There!"

"Where? I don't see anything," Jacki quipped, her chair scraping on the floor.

"Thought I saw a shadow right—backup a few seconds again." Clar kept peering at the wall, waiting for the replay of that section of the interview. "Clint, are you going...."

The room went dark and Clar stiffened. A hand, cold as ice, wrapped around her face from behind. A cloth covered her mouth and nose. Panic gripped her as the sickening smell pulled her down into a swirling drain of nothingness.

CHAPTER 13

Jimmy wove in and out of downtown traffic towards the 110 southbound until he hit exit 21 leading to Santa Monica and the beach. He needed to clear his head, and with the help of the salty air and waves crashing the shore, he'd be able to lose himself from this world—and all the crud.

He burned inside. Anger and disbelief fueling the fire. Of all the damn fool things to do, Clar had the nerve to tell him to get the hell out of her life. Well damn it, for once he'd do exactly that! She'd get what she wanted all these years...him gone.

He'd walk the hell away from her and her endless issues with life. He had enough shit of his own to figure out. Cameron being in LA only managed to conjure up Jimmy's past failed attempt at justice. He couldn't even begin to fathom how a low-down piece of sidewalk crud like Reed Cameron had turned over a new leaf. No way, no how.

Even for the reasons Cameron gave for being in LA, there had to be a catch.

There was always a catch. A leopard doesn't change its spots.

Clar's endless need to baby Levi, like he was totally incapable of doing so himself drove him crazy. Levi was a grown man, not a lost boy. Jimmy thought about a few of the scrapes Levi had been in. Well, maybe he was lost. What did she expect him to do? Fight law enforcement and find out who in the hell laid Levi up in a state of who knew what? To find out why a few of her candy wrappers were left at the scene? Figure out why the sicko wanted to lure Clar back to LA? Well, he wasn't going to do it. Clar and her posse could go in on their own and find the damn killer. He wanted no part of it...not anymore.

He'd disappear from the face of the earth just like his dad had. No word. No trace. No way for anyone to contact him. Go to work one day to never return. After all, the killer wasn't after Jimmy. No, the killer's target was Clar—plain and simple.

Jimmy sped past cars and landscape, his mind shaking off the painful image of his dad. The Chicago PD brass came to his house with some story about his dad going down in the line of duty. His mother cried for days until they laid Sean O'Brien in a six-foot hole as the family and the Chicago PD paid homage. Jimmy didn't buy the hero story back then any more than he did today. His dad deserted them, that's all he knew—all he remembered. He'd always sworn he'd never take the same easy route. So, what the hell was he doing running away?

Suddenly a vision of Clar, laying in a pool of blood, pink candy wrappers strewn over her violated body flashed through Jimmy's horrified mind. His shoulders tightened like an overwound clock. The muscles in his thighs twitched. His stomach convulsed. Good gawd, what the hell was he doing running away again, leaving her alone and vulnerable at a time like this?

"Fuck, not on my watch, you bastard!" Heart racing, Jimmy gripped the wheel then swerved into the far-right lane traffic, horns blasting one after the other. He sped up the nearest off ramp, over the bridge, then down the on ramp and headed north back on the 110. The rush hour traffic increased as he continued to weave in and out of vehicles; the drivers giving him the finger, and brakes squealing and horns honking like crazy. He didn't give a damn.

Jimmy punched the panel on his dash, "Call Detective Reed Cameron."

"Cameron." The gruff voice barked.

"Cameron, it's O'Brien." After a few seconds he could sense the man tensing up on the other end, but their petty differences didn't matter. "Cameron, you still there? Okay, so be the asshole you've always been and listen, don't talk. Meet me at Cum Again Studios. I've got a bad feeling." Jimmy's white knuckled grip tightened around the steering wheel, his stomach twisting in knots.

He had to get back to the studio.

He had to tell Clar he wasn't about to abandon her, not now, not ever. Unlike his father, Jimmy would come back to her no matter the situation. Jimmy had to tell her he'd love her through the end of time.

Ignoring the city speed limit, Jimmy ran a red light nearly crashing with a big black caddie. The driver hunched low over the steering wheel, gave him the finger. Tires screaming defiance, Jimmy ignored him and squealed into the studio driveway. Thank God, Jacki's car was still here, he was in time. He relaxed for a moment until he knew he still had something important to do, something he couldn't put off. He threw open his door seconds after the engine halted, then sprinted up the walk and into the reception area of the studio. The unnatural depth of the quiet hit him like a ton of bricks upon entering. Nothing moved, not even the air conditioning was running, only the thundering of his racing pulse split the quiet. It felt like a fricking ghost town. Where the hell was everyone? Why weren't they answering?

"Clar!" James called out; icy fear squeezed his heart until he thought he'd die. Glancing at the desk he noticed Jacki's notes and the DVR were missing. "Where is everyone?"

Maybe they're in the studio and can't hear me. Please, dear God, don't let me find her dead. The hairs on the back of his neck snaked over locked muscles. Jimmy swallowed the sour taste lingering in the back of his throat, then headed toward Studio A.

He clutched the doorknob, jumping out of his skin when the air conditioning unit kicked back to life. Pushing the door open, he peered into darkness. Light, hollow murmurs reached him, and he flicked on the light switch. His greatest fear slapped him in the face.

Across the room Jacki struggled to her feet using a toppled chair for support. Clint rolled over on his knees, then slowly stood up. In front of the projector, a long, blond wig lay in a heap on the floor.

Bending down, Jimmy snatched the bundle of blond hair up, grabbing a fluttering piece of paper freed from the tangled strands. The words formed on the page pierced his heart, then his soul. He looked from Jacki to Clint as he attempted to temper the rage burning through him.

"Where the hell is Clar?" A wave of cold, like an icy winter wind, hit his core as he demanded to know where she was. But Jimmy knew. It was plainly relayed in the message. The asshole had her and it was all Jimmy's fault. He should have stayed. Should have gotten a breath of fresh air, calmed down a bit, and then come back in to reason with Clar. But no, he had to jump in the truck like a spoiled little boy, tail tucked between his legs and run as far from what he desired most in life.

IF YOU WANT TO FIND YOUR PRECIOUS CANDY, COME WHERE TIME HAS BEEN FORGOTTEN.

Each letter perfectly formed with pieces of pink KK candy wrappers.

"What the fuck is going on?" Cameron's voice boomed through the room, shaking Jimmy out of his shocked state of mind. "Why are you holding that wig, O'Brien? Looking to amp up your style?"

"It's Clar's. She was wearing it earlier today and now she's been kidnapped," Jimmy hissed, glaring across the room at the two people he thought would have had her back. *Goes to show, don't do anything without first finding out if it works for all involved. And NEVER leave the one you love in the hands of two PIs! Love? Hell no! No more snap emotional decisions from this moment forward.* "We had a fight. I left. I came back to find these two yahoos struggling to their feet, and this on the floor with the wig." Jimmy handed Cameron the hand crafted, cryptic note. "And before you say it, yes, we went behind your back. Yes, it was stupid, dangerous, and out of line."

Cameron looked over the crumbled paper, his jaw clenching. "And this is the result of whatever it is that you have done here today. You of all people know I could throw you in jail for obstruction of justice. Now instead of finding a murderer, we've got a missing person on our hands. And that person is connected to not only the scene of the crime, but also the victim in this case." His tone sharp, Cameron waved the paper at all of them, shaking his head in disgust. "First off, what the hell happened here today? And don't leave a frickin' thing out of the equation."

"We held a mock interview with Kandi Kyses hoping to draw the killer out," Jacki quipped, massaging her temples in slow circles with the pad of her index fingers.

Clint rubbed the back of his neck, "Then this fuck got her pissed off, they had a few words, and he ran."

"In my defense, Clar told me to leave so I did!" Jimmy's gut rolled violently. He had pushed the envelope; it was what he did. Push until the truth comes out. Push until he'd finally beaten a horse dead. An instinct he didn't know how to control and now it had pushed Clar away.

"And that childish reaction has gotten us here. Unless Clar's in the bathroom, she's missing," Jacki piped in from the chair where she landed after crawling up from the floor. "Damn, my head feels like a jackhammer's inside."

"If I had to guess—we were KO'd by the killer." Clint piped in. "An invisible one, I might add."

"Since lover boy here is holding that wig,"—Cameron waved the now ransom note in the air, "and the fact this is here as well, it's a safe bet she's gone. What happened after the fight?"

"I left Clar in the care of these two Bozos. I was going to head to Santa Monica to clear my head, then decided no way in hell was I going to leave without knowing she was safe." Jimmy's shoulders slumped. He'd never tell them how he'd failed at protecting someone he cared about again. First his mother, after his father died, then the citizens of Chicago from a corrupt system. Now Clar. The vision of her lying in a pool of blood still fresh in his mind, he shivered slightly.

"Jimmy, did you know Evie had a brother?" Jacki asked, testing the floor beneath her feet. "Some guy came in right after you left looking for her."

Cameron looked up from his notes, his brows furrowed. "Did this 'brother' give his name?"

"Edward, Edward DeLuca," Jacki answered, reaching for her notes.

"Eddie, here in LA? Great." Cameron shook his head "That can't be good."

Jimmy crossed the room feeling like he waded through muck. Cameron knew something. How far could he press the detective this time? "So, he's back in town, or did he ever really leave?"

"According to what Mr. DeLuca said, Evie didn't know he was in town. He said she wasn't expecting him." Clint scowled, his eyes darting between Jimmy and Cameron. Jimmy knew that Ranger mind of his was fast at work, coming up with a million scenarios. "If you ask me, he's up to no good. There's something very unsettling about the guy. He's a bit too slick for my tastes."

"If he's here, something is up in Chicago. I'll make a few calls and see what I can find out." Cameron cocked his head, his face etched in thought. "What happened after he came in?"

"Not much, said he was looking for Evie and then he left. He did seem a bit star struck that he met 'Kandi' if that means anything." Jacki volunteered, gathering up the pages scattered on the floor. "I was going through Evie's computer files looking for any information when he came in right after Jimmy left."

"Is that the guy I passed when I left?" Jimmy asked, trying to recall the man he briefly rubbed shoulders with. Nothing that would make him stand out just in passing. Nothing about the guy would have made him think of Evie, either.

Clint nodded, helping Jacki pick up the papers. "A few minutes after Jimmy was out the door, we—Clar, Jacki, and myself—came in here to watch the interview on a bigger screen. We each took a third of the projection looking for anything remotely suspicious when Clar asked for a rewind because she thought she'd seen something. Next thing I knew I was crawling to my knees, Jacki was laying curled up on the floor, Clar's wig lay in a heap, and Jimmy had burst in guns blazing."

"That's where I came in and found them senseless. And Clar gone."

Cameron flipped through his notes, scowling. "You said he was looking for Evie? Wasn't she here?"

"No, she hadn't come in. In fact, never even called." Jimmy remembered how concerned

Clar was about Evie's mysterious absence. "Clar was a little concerned, surprised even that she hadn't even called in."

"Is that unusual?" Cameron pursed his lips, his eyebrows squished together.

"According to Clar, highly unusual," Jacki said.

"O'Brien, can you verify? You know her better than these two." Cameron wandered over to where Jacki sat with her papers neatly stacked on her lap, then turned and returned.

"Evie never missed a day. The studio is her lifeline if you ask me." Jimmy watched Cameron stare at the floor, nodding his head as if in answer to a question he only knew. "Listen, Evie may be a lot of things. Daughter of a mobster for instance and, Cameron, don't think we're not going to talk about that. I think she's had a rough life and she can be a hard person to deal with, but she'd never do anything to hurt this studio."

"Okay, that's it for now. I'll put a missing person, possible kidnapping, out on Clar Turner." Cameron snapped his notebook shut, pointing his finger at Jimmy. "O'Brien, since you have a history with Evie Dagmyer, I want you to come with me."

"I don't know how much she'll tell me, there's never been any love lost between us," Jimmy muttered. "But I'll do anything, talk to anyone, if it'll help find Clar."

Clar floated upon a fluff of cloud with a wisp of a breeze. Her mind peaceful, no ugly thoughts. No need to run and hide. She sighed and opened her eyes to darkness surrounding her. Panic replaced the tranquility. Nostrils flared, fear skipping through her. Clar struggled against the bindings to move her arms and legs, her head hitting something hard and unyielding, exploding with sharp pain. Tears stung her eyes. She let out a muffled scream through the blockage in her mouth, the taste resembling something of an old sock.

"If I were you, I'd settle down back there," a deep, mechanical voice warned. "I wouldn't want you to get hurt on the way, Kandi. No, that'll come later in a pleasurable way. I promise you, the pain will only last an instant, followed by pleasure, and then you'll be set free—and so will I."

The sinister laugh vibrated around her and she involuntarily shivered. Who was threatening her? Clar didn't recognize the voice, and her captor referred to her as Kandi, using her film name. Pushing fear aside, Clar focused on what her senses could tell her.

I'm in the back of a car and, shit, some deranged fan has me. Or it's the killer. Okay, don't panic.

Breathe in and out. Remember the self-defense Jacki taught you. Once this madman gets me out, I'm gonna take this sucker out! The vehicle sped over rough roads. It was obviously not paved, at least not a good one judging from the way she jostled about.

"Have no fear, my love, by now your friends are awake feeling the world has crashed down around them. They are probably wondering where you are and have called the authorities. Their speed, or lack of it, determines when they find you. Cops always act like they're on a movie set. Humph! No direction with law enforcement these days. A pity really, a family needs its army. And yours, Clar Turner, has finally been defeated!"

The arsenic laced words mingled with malice gripped her racing heart. A second involuntary cry escaped Clar. She quickly sucked down any further display of fright. A hard pill to swallow, fear finally dislodged from her mind.

He knows who I really am. I'm not going to give this asshole satisfaction. Whoever this lunatic is, I'm going to make sure he never sees the light of day. If I live long enough that is.

"In case you're curious, and I'm sure you are, I left a note with your wig. That reporter boyfriend of yours will eventually figure it out, along with that Chicago detective Cameron. Now that's one warped SOB." A sigh, followed by a chuckle floated over Clar. "It's a shame he's no longer on the wrong side of the law. Ah well, I'm sure by now your friends are sporting a few minor aches and pains from the gas, but don't worry, they'll recover." The vehicle slowed, the crunching of tires on gravel grated on Clar's spinning mind.

"I have to tell you something. Your full figure is so much more appetizing than that skinny one you sported at the height of your film career. I've found it does crazy things to my body. Leaving the business has been kind to you. I truly believe there's nothing sexier than gazing upon a body in its natural form, don't you agree? You'll make millions with your final performance drenched in nothing but chocolate as the camera fades to pink then black. Branding is everything, don't you think? Of course, you won't live long enough to collect the royalties. The studio will though, in your memory of course."

Clar's stomach churned, the sour bile fighting to find a way up and through her mouth. If the rumblings didn't settle down soon, she'd likely drown in her own vomit. She took deep breaths, one at a time, through her nose until the rolling ceased. At least for the time being.

"I think we've had enough conversation for now. I can only imagine how tired you must be and crave the need to rest."

The vehicle slid to a stop, slamming Clar between the seat and floorboards. The door Clar's head was lodged against swung open. The heat of the day washed over her. A sweet smell enveloped her nose and mouth. Clar fell back into the peaceful sleep she'd woke from several minutes before. The sound of evil laughter chasing her down the rabbit's hole.

CHAPTER 14

The silence in the car was deafening. Whatever was on Cameron's mind he kept close to the vest. When there's a cop in the car with something on his mind there's no time like the present for a journalist to start asking questions. Jimmy let out the deep breath he'd been holding since knowing he'd be the one responsible in getting Evie to talk. "Come on, Reed, what was so tough growing up a mobster's daughter? She grew up rich. The best of life at her fingertips. Evie had everything she'd ever need."

"Everything but the love of her father," Cameron huffed in disgust. "Reed? Since when are we on a first name basis, O'Brien?"

Jimmy shook his head, ignoring the bait. He wasn't about to dredge up old wounds with the detective, it was time to move past that. "Every daddy in the world loves their little girls. I find it hard to believe DeLuca didn't love Evie."

Cameron cast Jimmy a side glance, his lips pinched together. "Shows how much you know. Sal couldn't afford to have his mistress show up with his illegitimate daughter. It was enough that he'd taken Eddie under his wing and brought him into the family. Eddie is the only son Sal's ever had, legit or not. In my opinion, he desired his blood son take the reins when his time was over, and that won't be for a long time to come. For a 'former' crime boss, Sal is a health nut even if he isn't exactly Adonis."

"The Sal DeLuca I remember didn't appear to be the type to eat anything healthy. He's a pretty big man." Jimmy watched the buildings slide by. They were traveling on the 405 heading toward Evie's apartment on Wilshire near the Westwood district. He prayed they weren't on a path to nowhere, and that Evie would be home to answer some questions. Otherwise, the leads would be hard to unearth from this point on. Time was running out.

"In more ways than his physical appearance alone. It took a while to convince him to let me come out here. As strange as it may be, family means a lot to Sal. He knew I needed to find out who killed Dylan. One thing is certain, if it had been any of the DeLuca family, Sal would have had their heads on a spike." Cameron wove through the afternoon traffic, his grip visibly tightening around the wheel. Jimmy noted the control on the detective's face as he kept his emotions in check. "Sal wanted his son to become head of the family. I think when it came to Eddie, he was totally wrong. He's a canon ready to be ignited."

"If family means so much, then why hide his daughter and take Eddie with him?" Jimmy thought he already knew the answer, he needed to hear Cameron confirm it. DeLuca thought women were to be kept out of business, seen as weak links.

"Eddie is his only son. He convinced his wife that this boy needed his father, so he brought him home when he turned a year old—it took that long for Gianna to finally concede. She'd always wanted a boy since they already had three daughters. She couldn't have more children, and she truly loved Sal with all her heart. She knew of his mistress, Belle, and where Sal spent his nights when he didn't come home. When she finally gave in to her motherly instincts to give the child a better chance at life, it was on the condition that the mother and daughter would be tucked far away somewhere. He was to never have contact with the girl—or her mother ever again. Sal stayed true to his word. *He* never did have contact. Everything went through his consigliere until Gianna passed.

"Evie and her mother were kept tucked away in northern Wisconsin. Presents arrived at the appropriate time. A generous deposit was made each month into Belle's bank account. The poor little girl dressed in hand me downs a few sizes too big. Afraid of having Sal take her daughter from her, Belle made sure Evie didn't draw attention to herself by not having the best of everything. When Evie grew up enough to understand who her father was, she'd send messages back to him through the consigliere. After college, she begged Sal to let her go to California to live. He set her up at the studio as a receptionist, with the promise when the time came, she would be able to take the business over, if she proved herself to have a good head for business." Cameron's smile spread to the corners of his eyes. There was a sense of pride that surprised even Jimmy.

"And that time is drawing nearer, prompting Eddie's sudden appearance in her life," Jimmy confirmed, knowing Evie had a head for business that out matched any man. She'd proven herself with the studio. Even after Dylan's death, she cut staff and screened everyone who walked through the doors.

"I'm afraid so. Evie's smart and knows more about running a business than Eddie ever could. The studio has thrived under her behind the scenes leadership. Then the studio took a hit following the murder of Dylan. Now the attack on Levi, not to mention Clar's candy wrappers, I'm not sure it can withstand the blow. There's a fox in the hen house and it doesn't look good in my opinion." Cameron sneered, taking the next exit onto Wilshire Boulevard. "Look, I know Evie can be many things, but a murderer she's not. Belle made sure she didn't know about what her father did for a living for a reason. She raised her right. I'm unclear as to how she found out, unless it was at Belle's funeral when Sal showed up to pay his respects. I know they had an old-fashioned father-daughter talk about her education and future."

"How does Eddie fit into the picture? Wouldn't the family business be handed down to one of Sal's sons-in-law?" Jimmy tried to sort it all out. Could they have been jealous of one another? Did they ever know each other existed before now? That they were twins? Hell, it could be all of the above making for a deadly pack of dynamite.

Cameron let out a big whoosh of air. "That's where it gets interesting. None of Sal's legitimate daughters want anything to do with the 'family' business. They and their husbands distanced themselves. Sal loves his children with all his heart, even his illegitimate twins. Since the legitimate girls have shunned the business, that leaves either Eddie or Evie. Secretly, I think he was pleased with the disinterest.

"While Eddie has street smarts, Evie has the formal business education. Sal hoped they'd work together one day since they each brought something to the table, but Eddie being here is a bad omen. As far as I know, up until his appearance here in LA, he's never made contact with his older twin."

Jimmy mulled the information over in his head. Either Evie and Eddie are working together, or one of them is out to get the other. Either way, the conclusion he came up with couldn't have a happy ending. Someone was going to get hurt by greed. And Clar was caught in the middle of it all. "Which could mean Sal's either on his last legs, or about to be."

"Sadly, I think you're correct. Which is why we need to get to Evie's condo before Eddie does. If they are protecting each other, who knows what has happened to any evidence we may never find." Cameron sighed, pulling over to the curb. "There's one more thing, I know you think

Sal had something to do with Clar's parents' deaths. He didn't, but I think I may know who did. And I think it was the same person who had Dylan killed and put the hit out on Levi."

"One of the twins." Jimmy's stomach fell like a boulder in a landslide when Cameron nodded his head. The clock just sped up and they had no time to lose.

Jimmy quickly scanned the mailboxes, looking for Evie's condo apartment number. "She's on the sixth floor, 6B. And there's a DeLuca on the tenth floor in one of the penthouse suites."

"Now, that's interesting. Why would Eddie buy a condo in LA in the same building as his sister?" Cameron licked the end of the ever-present pencil, then jotted down some notes on his pocket size spiral notepad. "I'm going out on a limb, by presuming it is Eddie. The likelihood of it being some other DeLuca is a very slim chance by my estimation."

"With no first name or initial it's a presumption I'm willing to make." Jimmy pressed the elevator up button, his heart racing while waiting for the doors to swoosh open. "I'm guessing Evie may have to verify that question." *Here we go, I hope she's in a cooperative mood and not her usual snarky one.* Jimmy looked over at Cameron and shook his head in amusement.

"Why don't you come into the twenty-first century and use a tablet like everyone else, instead of scratching your notes in that pocket sized spiral?" Wiping away the nervous perspiration from his upper lip, Jimmy sucked in a deep breath. He had a feeling about Evie, and it wasn't a good one. He needed a distraction to calm his pounding pulse down.

"Because I know my notes are my own and not out on a cloud in someone else's air space." Cameron looked up from the paper, scowling at Jimmy. "You never have said how you and Clar Turner became so close."

"Hadn't I? I didn't realize the level of our relationship was pertinent information to this case." Jimmy glanced at Cameron, a sliver of a chill creeping up his spine. "What's your interest, Cameron? Because she's Karl Turner's daughter?"

The doors slowly swished open. Jimmy entered, pushing the button for the sixth floor. Not exactly penthouse level, but with only ten floors to the building, still not a bad view. He doubted Evie was into the view of LA from her balcony.

"Humph, that's exactly what I've been wondering about you, O'Brien. What's your motive in keeping Ms. Turner close to you? Is it strictly personal? Or are you looking for something?" Cameron accused, quickly surveying the entryway that led back to Wilshire as the doors closed. "Bad cops and judges weren't the only people on Turner's list."

His relationship with Clar was none of Cameron's business. Hell, there were times when Jimmy didn't even feel it was any of his own business. He wasn't sure how Clar felt, but he'd been head over heels for her from the start. Long before he knew she was Karl Turner's daughter.

Karl Turner had been the one to tip him off about the mayor and his connection to the DeLuca family. His long list of cops, district attorneys, and other officials was never found. Even after his death, the tell all list haunted those whose names were scrolled on the paper. A reporter never gave up his resources, even the dead ones.

The elevator slid in silence to the sixth floor and the doors opened to an average looking hall. Nothing special. Plain and simple like Evie. They continued down the hall, coming to unit 6B. Jimmy reached out, knocking on the door.

"Evie, it's Jimmy O'Brien." He waited a moment then knocked a bit harder. "Evie?" It was quiet—deathly quiet. Jimmy looked over at Cameron, then reached for the doorknob. The detective's large hand clasped tightly around

Jimmy's wrist, pulling it away from the gold tone globe.

"Best to have my prints on there; just in case it turns out to be a crime scene." Cameron released his hold and turned the knob, surprised when the door opened. "Would she leave it unlocked?"

"I don't think it's in her DNA to give anyone the opportunity to have a glimpse into her private life, Cameron. So no, I don't believe she would for a second." Jimmy walked through the door, calling out. "Evie! Are you here?"

They stalked into the sparsely furnished living room, then through the simple dining, and finally the sterile white kitchen. "It doesn't look like she's been here for a while. Not a dirty dish in the place," Cameron noted, pulling open the dishwasher door.

"Shhh!" Jimmy tilted his head, then walked back into the living room, looking down the hallway toward the bedrooms and bathroom. A dull whimper crept softly into his senses. "Did you hear something?" He cocked his head again, listening, watching, waiting.

"No."

"Evie, are you here? It's Jimmy," Jimmy called out, ignoring Cameron. Jimmy took a few soft steps down the hall. The whimper, a little louder than before, snuck out from its hiding place. "There! I heard it again." He ran down the hall, throwing open the first door he'd come to. The bathroom, nothing. Not even a bath towel hung up to dry.

"Evie, I'm coming in." Jimmy pushed open a bedroom door and ran into the room. "Cameron, I found her!"

Evie lay on the bed, hands bound behind her back, ankles shackled to a bedpost, and a piece of gray tape strapped tightly across her mouth. Tears glossed over the frightened wild animal gaze. Toppled across the top of the bedside table were several bottles of prescription medications, their contents safe inside.

"I'm sorry, but this might sting." Jimmy grabbed a corner of the tape and pulled quickly making her squeal in pain.

"I'm gonna kill that SOB!" Evie spat with the venom of a poisonous snake as she struggled against the restraints.

"Evie, first things first. You need to stay still." Jimmy worked slowly to untie her hands, hoping she'd calm down a bit. The more she pulled against the knots, the tighter they'd become. Whoever did the knot work knew exactly what they were doing. "Who did this do you?"

"My fucking brother!" Evie said, seconds before the tears flowed unabated down her cheeks.

⌒⌒

"Are you sure you want to do this? It could be a wild goose chase, Evie." Jimmy held firm his grip of Evie's arm, keeping her steady on the way down the hall to the elevator. The stubborn woman wouldn't let either Jimmy or Cameron call paramedics. No, Evie wanted to confront her brother with what he'd done to her. Cameron, for some crazy reason Jimmy couldn't figure out, went along with it, leaving Jimmy to stall as long as possible. Maybe it was out of Cameron's sense of loyalty to DeLuca; it was the only option remotely making any sense. As long as it led to getting Clar back he didn't give a damn what the reasons were. The next forty-eight hours were crucial if they were going to find her alive—and they'd wasted enough time already.

An image of Clar tied and shackled in a similar fashion to the way they found Evie flashed through Jimmy's mind. Then a naked Clar spread out like a sacrificial lamb flashed into the recesses of his brain. His heart sped with panic. The hand clasped around Evie's arm flexed tightly. *You son-of-a-bitch, I'll kill you if you hurt her!*

"Hey, not so damn tight!" Evie glared at him, then yanked her arm from his grasp, hissing her reply. "That SOB is as dead to me as a squashed bug. Even if this isn't his condo, daddy and I are going to have a sit-down heart-to-heart about brother dearest. If Eddie lives long enough.

"After spending the past twenty-four hours with baby brother yapping nonstop about how he's the rightful heir to the kingdom, I think Eddie plans on destroying, or even, killing me. Daddy isn't in the best of health. Several years ago, the family consigliere sent word for me to be prepared to take over the West Coast properties. Eddie has been tending to the Chicago investments where he can be monitored. To say he's been an unhappy camper is an understatement. He wants both the West and Chicago arenas." Evie drew in a breath then looked up at Jimmy with tearful eyes, catching him off guard with the love reflected in them.

"He's always been a wild card. Momma said the moment he popped out, Eddie did nothing but scream and throw tantrums. I think that's why daddy took him to live with him. Momma wouldn't have been able to handle both Eddie and I. We don't have the normal twin tendencies. I don't know who Eddie has become. How he thinks. What he feels. He's a complete stranger to me." The sadness in Evie's words took Jimmy by surprise. The tough nut does have a soft spot after all.

While Cameron had gone ahead of them to obtain the proper forms to legally gain entry into the penthouse condo, Jimmy continued to talk Evie down from her anger. He bet the odds she had been more scared than angry at first—it hadn't taken long for those feelings to be reversed.

The elevator doors slid open revealing a hallway of lush white carpeting and priceless paintings adoring the walls in gold frames. Poised at the end of the corridor, a boldly designed door with inlaid vines and grapes gleamed like a shiny sentry, reminding Jimmy of a door leading to a Greek god.

Everything about the floor said someone with way too much money who loved flaunting it lives here. Four floors below, where Evie lived, felt like a different world. Jimmy decided he liked Evie's choice of modest living, compared to the extravagance he had a feeling they were about to walk into.

The unlocked door swung open to an expansive living room decorated in whites and muted gold. The elegantly simple furniture screamed of richness and excess. A few things caught Jimmy's eye. The full wall of glass panel doors leading out to the balcony with an impressive view of downtown LA, and the wall mural painted with soft hues. The room, while elegant, felt lonely and cold.

"Pretty impressive, isn't it?" Cameron closed the door, his eyes glittering with envy.

"If you like this sort of thing." Jimmy toured the room, glancing at the book titles in the case. "Humph, I'll bet he's never read one of these—they're all classics."

"Shows what you know," Evie huffed. "My brother loves the classics, as well as period novels from the twenties. He felt it was a way for him to understand daddy's business, even if the old ways are, well, old. He made sure I knew about his collection of first editions. It obviously makes him feel important or something."

Jimmy glanced into the kitchen littered with dishes and various frozen meal boxes. He opened the door to the bathroom and smiled. *Well, at least he's a typical guy. Doesn't hang up a towel even to save his own skin.*

"Holy shit!"

Down the hall, standing in the doorway of the last bedroom, Cameron stood motionless. Jimmy jogged toward him, praying to the Almighty that a dead body was not in that room. Pushing passed Cameron, Jimmy halted in his tracks and stared.

Surrounding the headboard on the wall were several movie poster size pictures of Dylan, Levi, Evie...and Clar. Dylan's face had been slashed with red paint. Levi's photo had a huge yellow question mark on it. Neither Clar and Evie's pictures were marked, but it was all too clear they were next on the list.

On the connecting wall where an expensive Monet painting had hung but now lay propped against a bedside table, was a map the size of the queen size bed. A bright yellow circle with a long tail attached to it looked like a yellow balloon taking flight. Jimmy touched the yellow tail, following its trail with his finger. The tail went from Wilshire north on the 405. The balloon encompassed the City of Santa Clarita and the surrounding area.

"I think I know where he's gone." Jimmy scoured the room, looking for anything that they may have missed. He walked over to one of the bedside tables, pulling open a drawer. His heart stuttered for a moment and he thought he'd died in that instant.

"He's taken Clar to the West Canyon Movie Ranch." Jimmy pulled the printed website information about the ranch out of the drawer. "It's a location north of Santa Clarita with old movie sets on about a hundred acres. And he's got at least an hour head start on us."

CHAPTER 15

Clar slowly rose from the depths of her foggy mind. Her eyes ached. Her head pounded with a dull thump. It was as though she just awakening out of a drunken stupor. A shadow moved toward her. "Where am I?"

The shadow moved further away. "Jimmy?" Clar blinked heavy eyelids, fighting to stay near the light. Darkness beckoned her to fall back into its depths.

"No, not that washed up newspaper man." The voice held a ring of familiarity to it. Clar strained to focus on the shadow's outline.

"Ah, the queen of porn is coming back to life. Sadly, I can't have you fully awake, my dear, what fun would that be? You should be attentive just enough to feel pleasure, the kind of pleasure felt when fans watch your movies."

Clar twitched at the prick of a needle going into her arm. A mesh blindfold obstructed her already murky vision.

"Don't worry, my love. I'm not going to hurt you—yet. I do want you to be somewhat cognizant of the scene. An actress must know who her leading lady is, shouldn't she?"

"Why...are...you...doing...this?" Clar started to slip into a place somewhere between sleep and being alert. Peering weakly into the shadows, she barely made things out. The setting sunlight scarcely came through a door, casting fading rays on brown and white tiles. Clar turned her head slowly and focused on a nearby bar and some tables and chairs before the blurriness returned.

"Why she asks. It's very simple, my dear. You've been a thorn in my side I plan to eliminate once and for all. The sex queen dethroned. A new queen will sit upon the throne."

Clar licked her lips with what little moisture left in her mouth. Her upper body rose and moved. Clar's lower half followed feeling like a ton of logs being dragged along behind. Her concentration diminished by the second.

Her bottom plopped down in a seat. Her arms felt like mush as they were raised and attached to something cold and rough above her head.

"Humph! Okay, this will do for the time being. You've gained a bit more weight than I thought since you retired, Kandi."

The shadow floated across her impaired vision, and she was barely able to follow it through the dark mesh of the mask. Clar made out the hazy figure. Her heart skipped a beat. Her veins pulsed with rushing blood. The familiarity of the voice finally registered. The voice sounded like Evie's, but Clar couldn't remember if she'd been in the front seat of the car or not.

"Evie, is that you?"

The shadow moved closer, but only as near as the fringes of the fading light. "All these years I've watched every shoot, every movie, as men came crawling to you all longing and dewy eyed. Do you know how many times I imagined strong and powerful hands caressing me every night as I fell into a fantasy world of lust? No, of course not." The words were mechanical and filled with crawling dread. She appeared to be on the brink of collapse in the ill-fitting clothing hanging from her frame. She continued to stare at the ceiling with a dullness filled with scorn and jealousy. In the paling light, her gaze shifted back to Clar.

"Sexual adventures happened to everyone else in the bars, clubs, cafes, even on the street. I became obsessed to be one of those having all the fun I'd been missing out on. Then I realized, I needed to stop trying to be perfect. To stop trying to be Kandi Kyses, because I'm not like you at all. No matter how much I tried, no one would want to bed someone who looks like me.

"A frumpy girl with the unruly, mousy brown hair and plain face to match. Hell, even make-up and seductive clothing didn't help unless the target was drunk as a skunk and the place was dark. It's true you know, girls like me do get prettier at closing time." Laughter filled the room then stopped abruptly. The atmosphere turned icy cold. "It's the legacy daddy left me when he planted his seed deep in mama's womb."

In the increasing shadows, a fingertip slid over Clar's exposed breast with a strange intimacy. Clar shivered. Then the caress was gone.

"I've always wondered what it was like to be Kandi Kyses. To have a strong intimacy with your co-stars, or friends like Levi and Dylan. But they wouldn't have me. Dylan didn't think I was pretty enough. Levi doesn't think I'm male enough.

"He was a mistake you know—Levi. I should have let the hit man take care of that business, but I wanted him all to myself. To make him pay for his rejection."

Clar licked her parched lips, mustering up what was left of her disappearing consciousness and courage. "Evie, believe me. You don't want that life at all. It's not as glamorous as you think. The men who watch those movies are looking at the actors as an object of lust. There's someone for everyone out there. He'll show up one day and give you more love than you could imagine because you are you, not some painted up wanna be. You just have to keep your eyes and ears open to love." *Like Jimmy has shown me all these years, and I push him away each time.* Tears filled Clar's eyes, and all she could do was let them fall beneath the mask and down her cheeks.

Yes, she did love him. Needed him. Wanted him. If she got out of this nightmare, she'd show him how much.

"That's easy for you to say, you've never had to fight for something or to have someone love you." Her voice softened for a moment, then she shuffled back deeper into the shadows and out of Clar's masked sight. Something scraped against the floor like fingernails across a chalkboard.

Clar swallowed gathering her wits over quaking fear. "That's where you are wrong. My parents were killed in a car accident when I was in college. They were on their way to see me! How do you think that makes me feel? It was my fault they died. Dad never got to enjoy his police retirement at all."

"It's not the same. They loved you. My father shipped me off. He didn't want to be seen with me, to protect my mother and I, so he said. All I wanted was his love, and he denied me."

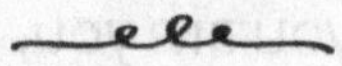

"Even after I had put the hit out on that cop, my father still didn't get it. No one knows I did it. Hell, I had no choice. I had to save the DeLuca empire." Eddie sat back in a chair enjoying the effect of his words registering across his hostage's face. Even behind the blindfold, he could feel the fear in Clar's eyes at they bore into him, the fierce anger as she realized what he was hinting at. *Damn, even as a hostage she's beautiful. Too bad it has to end this way. I'd much rather take my time and give my cock a taste of her. No time to think about that now. Get the job done here and back in LA. Then one more wrinkle to iron out and it'll all be mine.*

"W-w-what cop?"

Eddie smiled, knowing the fish was his—hook, line, and sinker. "You know, the one from Chicago who had a file listing the names of all of father's informants and payroll. It included cops and public officials on the take. Even had a few newspaper men's names on it. It's the one that wasn't found in the wreck that day in California by my men.

"I thought I'd had it planned to a tee. Thought Dead Man's Curve was the best place in California for the accident. I'd underestimated Turner though. He'd done something with the fucking list before he packed up and headed west. I've never been able to find it. Maybe it burned up. Maybe it didn't. I need to know for sure which it is."

"Noooooo!" Clar's sobs sent a rush of ecstasy through Eddie. Something about a cry of pain turned him on. Ever since he'd made his first kill as a toddler, he felt the excitement. That's why momma let Sal take him away to live with him at the compound. Thought being with his father would take care of Eddie killing everything in sight, including helpless insects, rodents, even a baby bird now and then. It worked up to the formidable teen years. At sixteen he found out what would happen to the family business once Sal died. Eddie heard the discussion of Sal's will with the family consigliere one night. The business would be split between him and Evie.

The desire to kill something began to fill him once more.

"The way I see it, the cop's daughter might have that piece of paper and not even know it." Eddie presumed Turner had left the list to Clar. "And we both know that daughter would be you, Clarice Turner. At first, I thought you might have it stashed away in your house of chocolate, which by the way are the damn best melt in your mouth things I've ever tasted." Clar might not know she has it, but he'd bet it was stashed away amongst the papers her parents might have kept tucked away. It was those files he needed to get his hands on in order to complete his mission once he had the information. He'd finish with Clar, get back to LA and take care of big sister. Then hop on a plane back to Chicago and give Sal the bad news about Evelyn Dagmyer's accidental death by overdose.

Yes, there will be tears, sadness, and someone sent to bring the body back to Chicago for a bad ass private funeral. Everyone would come to pay their respects to the dead, and to Sal DeLuca. Soon enough after, they'd be paying their respects to Eddie Dagmyer DeLuca, the new head of the DeLuca family.

"I don't know about any list. Dad never discussed police business with the family. He felt it was unethical."

"That's funny. Karl Turner had the power to destroy every city official in Chicago from the mayor's office to the DA to the local garage mechanic." Eddie chuckled. "Tell me where you put all his papers, Clar, and all this will end. That file is the very thing that destroyed Jimmy O'Brien's newspaper career—or would have if Reed Cameron hadn't convinced Sal to cut him some slack."

"Jimmy? What does Jimmy have to do with this?"

"Father has a soft spot where Cameron is concerned. They go way back to growing up in the old neighborhood. Sal can't say no to Cameron unless there was good reason. So, he let him step away from family business to come out to sunny California to find his nephew's killer. That's one hit man who disappeared within days of Dylan Cameron's death—I made sure of it.

"Jimmy O'Brien was Turner's link to expose the corrupt mayor of being on the take and linked to the family. O'Brien should be at the bottom of the river not surfing around the California beaches. If not for Cameron he'd have been fish meat. I hate loose ends, and you, my sexy morsel, are a loose end I intend to tie up myself. Well, at least here at this location."

Eddie shuffled out the door, taking a glance up and down the street of the abandoned movie set. Nothing, not even a particle of dust stirred. Tugging on the ill-fitting women's clothing he'd taken from Evie's closet, he smiled to himself. Confident he was safe, he pulled off the long, unkempt, mousy brown wig that made him look more like Evie than he cared to admit. He'd be able to finish the job without any complications, and get back to LA before anyone suspected him. Then he'd take care of his sister once and for all. No more pussy footing around with the bitch.

"It's getting dark, and that fucked up detective and no good news reporter haven't made it here yet," Eddie said to himself, then turned, walked back in, and flipped on a light. The dim yellow glow cast eerie shadows around Clar and he snickered, "Well, I guess that means it's just you and me, babe."

"Don't call me babe! Call me by my given name, damn you, Evie. You know what it is after all these years of signing my film contracts and paychecks—use it!" Clar's head jerked from side-to-side searching for him. Eddie slid in behind her, keeping out of the light. He leaned in, a breath away from her ear and whispered in his well-practiced imitation of Evie.

"Oh yes, I know who you are. Where you live. I've tasted your delicious chocolates. Been in your house. Bought items from the town farmer's market. Watched you walk to the post office with boxes of chocolates tucked under your arm. You're Karl Turner's daughter. I believe you have the file and I'm going to have fun getting its location from you."

—ele—

Clar cocked her head, chasing away the hot breath on her ear. "I don't remember you ever ordering anything, Evie, let alone come into my home." She was positive no one from California she knew had stepped foot in her sleepy little town. Hell, Jimmy never once attempted to contact her. Levi, well Levi was too busy with his film schedule, calling when he had time or there was a crisis. Jacki had a ranch to run, so she gave Clar the space she needed to start a new life. They were the only ones she would ever expect to show up, if so inclined to do so.

And Evie? There's no way in hell Evie would ever leave LA just to spy on her. Her devotion to the studio was phenomenal, if not a bit overzealous for a receptionist.

"Who said anything about Evie? I know I didn't." The words a deep sinister tickle down the back of her neck sent chills racing down her spine. It felt as if evil had just touched her.

Clar shivered inwardly as fingers skirted down her arms, trailed lightly over her breasts, then clasped around her throat. She went still, holding her breath for a moment. The pressure was slight, almost sexual in nature. Was this how Dylan died? Had this psychopath toyed with Dylan before ending his life? Where the hell were the cops when you needed them?

"Remember when you looked at that little storefront on Lake Street a few months back? The one that once housed a coffee shop? I liked that one, small and manageable, very intimate."

Clar cringed as something moved through her hair and across her scalp.

Fingertips caressed every pressure point in her head. She lost to the sensation of letting released tension swarm over her shoulders down to her waist, settling in further below her belly button. Her stretched arms relaxed slightly. The pain from lack of blood flow danced through them, reminding her how immobile she really was.

"You need to relax. A good head massage will help, but who has the time for such luxuries?"

The manipulating digits ceased, leaving their burning mark on her scalp.

"If you're not Evie, then who the hell are you?" Clar swallowed the rancid tasting bile at the back of her throat. If she were to die today, she at least wanted to know by whose hands. "Or are you nothing more than a coward hiding in the shadows?"

"So, you are of the opinion that I'm a coward. Why? Because I might hire people to do my killing for me? In some ways you may be right, even though I do enjoy taking the life of helpless creatures."

"You're about to ruin your life for a piece of paper? Why?" Clar shifted her butt on the chair, transferring the muscle ache from one cheek to another. "Explain it to me so I can understand why you think this is all worth it. Why you think ending my life is worth a list of names." *Please hurry and find me, Jimmy. I don't know how much longer I will survive. Lord, please let me live long enough to tell him how much I love him. That's all I ask for.*

"It's not so much the names as it is taking what belongs to me. I've killed to protect the family. Hell, I'll kill today to protect it."

"Family are people who love you and you love back." Clar swallowed the lump of fear in the back of her throat. Maybe if she appealed to a love of family, she might convince her kidnapper to take off the blindfold.

"Yes, if you are talking about a father and mother, or brother and sister. I'm talking about a business, an enterprise older than either of us. One that should rightfully be mine, not some California transplant diva wannabe."

Who the hell can that be referring to—me? "How many have you killed to protect the family?"

"Directly? Or indirectly?"

"Does it matter? Killing is killing whether you do it by your own hand or you hire someone to do it for you?" Clar drew a breath, wetting her lips with the tip of her tongue. She could use a drink of water, anything to quench the thirst building.

"Hmmm, I see your point."

"At least directly your victim can see into your eyes. See what kind of person has decided to take their life for no good reason," Clar jabbed, wanting the menace behind her to come round and face her one on one. "Only a coward uses a blindfold to hide themselves from their victim. A coward who doesn't want to see their true reflection in the eyes of another as the light of life goes out."

"Shows what the fuck you know!" The body pressed in along her back. She stiffened at the feel of something familiar pressed against her spine, and she didn't think it was a weapon of any kind. It was a cock, a very large and hard piece of man flesh.

A man! This asshole is a man and he sounds like Evie enough for me to think it was her.

Fingers pulled at the ties of the mask, loosening it slightly. Clar tried to peek under it, but all she could see was the darkness of the meshed blindfold. Another eighth of an inch and Clar might get lucky. She'd have a better opportunity of escaping if she could see, and get a good measure of her captor. She needed time to put those damn self-defense skills to work!

CHAPTER 16

LAPD

"We've got no time to sit around waiting for a search warrant from a judge, Cameron! We've got to get out to that damn movie set before dark." Jimmy paced the room, shuffling through the various pictures of abandoned movie sets. It would take some time for them to figure out which set Eddie DeLuca was holed up in. It was time he wasn't willing to waste when it came to Clar's life.

"Who said anything about waiting around, Jimmy?" Jacki stood next to him, rocking back on her heels, hands tucked into her jean pockets. "Clint and I have been working out a plan, and I think it'll work. At least I hope it'll work. All we need is the search warrant to make it all nice and legal."

"And that plan would be what exactly? The longer we sit around here the chances of finding Clar dead, if at all, increases." Jimmy stopped by the window, looking out past the San Rafael Mountains. Somewhere north of that mountain range, on the edge of the Los Padres National Forest outside of Santa Clarita, a maniac held the woman he loved hostage. Everything they'd found in Eddie DeLuca's condo indicated his killing wouldn't end with Clar. Eddie DeLuca had a screw loose.

Pictures of Dylan Cameron with a big red X painted across them filled part of a wall. A date, written under a drawn happy face, marked his death on a promo shot taken during Dylan's last film. Lined up next were photos of Levi in all his naked glory; no X, no happy face, no date. Eddie had failed at that killing or had Levi been a pawn on this trail of death? It was the next group of pictures that haunted Jimmy most.

In a random order, half the wall was covered with pictures of Clar in Wisconsin. Clar at the park eating lunch. Clar making candy in her kitchen. Clar looking at real estate property last winter. Clar at the produce section of the local grocery store. Clar meeting Jacki at LAX. Clar with Jimmy at his beach house.

The words whore, slut, prostitute, or bitch were written over them in blood-red ink. Candy wrappers framed each photo—pink and black striped wrappers with a K scrolled on them.

There were even several photos of "Kandi" with Evie taken on one of the sets. Most of the photos looked as if the two were having an argument, as they sometimes did. A few appeared more pleasant, but not by much. How had Eddie DeLuca gotten into the studio without his sister knowing he was there? Had he posed as one of the camera men? Was he a master of disguise who altered his appearance? Was this how he'd planned to frame his sister and the reasons why she'd take her own life, with his help? Whoever he was, Eddie DeLuca had flown well under everyone's radar.

Also found was a copy of Sal DeLuca's will which indicated Evie would inherit all of the California investments and be under the advisement of the family consigliere. Eddie on the other hand, would only acquire the Chicago properties and be fully watched over by DeLuca's most trusted friend—Reed Cameron. Both Evie's and Cameron's names were crossed out in the same shade of blood red ink used on Clar's photos.

"Now just one minute here. If any of you go up there ready to bust up the joint you've got another thing coming. I'll throw the lot of you in jail for obstruction of justice, trespassing, and anything else I can drum up." Cameron stood behind his desk; the evidence they'd gathered from Eddie's condo scattered across the top of it. "This will sound odd coming from me but hear me out. If we don't do this right, and by right, I mean to the letter of the law, someone is going to get hurt. Or killed. I'll not have another person lose their life to this nut case."

"You're damn right! It can be Eddie DeLuca as far as I'm concerned." Jimmy stopped pacing, his mind turning over every possibility as the hour ticked away. It would take approximately an hour, if the traffic was good, to drive up to Santa Clarita. By now people should be home, eaten dinner with their families, and hopefully sitting in front of their TV's watching the next episode of their favorite program. Then again, this was LA and the freeway was always jammed no matter the time of day.

"Wolfe, you and this ranger friend of yours keep an eye on this hot head." Cameron pointed at Jimmy and shoved some of the evidence into a folder. "The last thing I need, O'Brien, is you running off and doing something stupid. I'm going to go see the judge right now and get him to sign this search warrant." Cameron didn't wait for a response, he grabbed the files and headed out the door.

Jimmy watched as Cameron shot through the scattered detectives' desks and into an elevator. No way on God's green earth was he waiting around for Cameron to return with, or without, that warrant. He had a plan of his own and it didn't include doing nothing. He looked over at Jacki and Clint, their heads huddled together. "Okay, so what the hell are we going to do?"

"As soon as Cameron gets back with the warrant, we go up there. Not a moment before. I'll not be part of an illegal search with or without my badge," Clint informed them from his corner of the room. Up until that point he'd been as silent as a church mouse, his face stone cold. Now a smile played at the corners of his mouth "Then I'll help you take the SOB down."

"I can't imagine how Evie's feeling right now. Her twin seems hell bent on framing her for the killings." Jacki shuffled through the discarded pictures, tossing them into a chair. "And Clar, she better be in one piece. She was top of my class, you know. That natural cop sense is in her, and it'll serve her well as long as she can keep DeLuca in line."

Time was getting shorter to find her alive. If there was one thing he and Evie agreed upon, it was that the cops wouldn't be of much help. Even Cameron, who'd been caught between the mob and the law, wanted to do this one by the book. Now that he found his nephew's killer, correction, the person likely responsible for Dylan Cameron's death, he wasn't going to let them do anything to jeopardize getting Eddie DeLuca in prison.

Jimmy had an ace in the hole the others didn't know about. Evie said she was friends with the owner of the movie set property. An old friend of her father's. Someone who would do anything for the DeLuca family within the parameters of the law, if asked.

Come on, Evie, give me something here. Any small bit of hope will do.

Jimmy's phone vibrated and he pulled it from his pocket. "I've got to go to the studio. Call me as soon as Cameron has the search warrant." With phone in hand, he headed to the elevator opening the text message from Evie.

"Pulled some strings. Called in a favor. Be at the movie set ranch asap."

ON THE WAY

Jimmy pressed the reply button on his phone keypad. Evie had come through after all. He had a clear path to the entry of the old movie sets. Finally, he felt like he was doing something other than twiddling his thumbs, waiting for justice to be served.

He was on his way to find Clar. To tell her he'll never let her go again.

Never was a long time—and he meant everything it implied to his dying day and beyond.

· ✦ ·

Driving through the Hollywood Hills, Jimmy thought of what he'd do once he got his hands on Clar. His mind flashed everything imaginable into his senses. Kiss her silly. Scold her for getting into her present situation. Apologize for being a fool and rushing off like an idiot. Cry like a baby. Hold her close, checking every part of her body for injuries until he was satisfied she was in one piece. Make love to her until the cows came home—in other words, forever.

He sped past Universal City where the Hollywood division of Universal Studios called home. For the first time since being exiled to California, he wanted normal. A normal day filled with normal people going about their normal lives. Not that there weren't any here in California, there were, but not in his circle of friends. They were all in the business. The film business that had him wondering when the acting stopped and real life took over.

A wife, kids, and a home with a dog running around the yard. Jimmy wanted that dream with Clar.

Miles and miles of highway edged with neighborhoods or businesses couldn't keep his mind off Clar.

The phone panel in his Durango sang out loud and clear. Jimmy glanced at the name flashing at him: "Reed Cameron."

"Shit!" Jimmy scanned the road side for a sign to the next town. He had only seconds to decide whether to answer the call or not. Reluctantly, he pressed the accept call button. "Cameron, what do you want? I'm in the midst of checking out leads for a story."

"Where the hell are you? Wolfe said you got a call and had to go to the studio. You are NOT at the station—I called," Cameron hissed, his anger more than evident by the tone of his voice. "I told you to stay here, not drive off to Santa Clarita."

Jimmy glanced at a sign indicating Santa Clarita was only miles away. On the other side of the canyon sprawled various movie sets. In one of those movie towns Clar was in trouble. "How do you know where I am, Cameron? Psychic, are you?"

"No, Evie Dagmyer called me. She said that you might be on your way up there; that she couldn't get a hold of me earlier."

"And you believe that story?" Jimmy smiled; glad Evie at least tried to cover her ass.

"That you are on your way there? Yes. That she couldn't get a hold of me? Hell no!"

"I'm going through Santa Clarita now. I'm not waiting for you to get up here, Cameron, so you better saddle up and get here before I kill that SOB once I get my hands on him." Jimmy turned up West Canyon Road and disconnected the call. Passing a mobile home park, blood rushed through his body. Energy sparked to life.

On the other side of these manufactured homes was Clar.

Jimmy drove slowly up to the open gate. When no one was there to wave him in, he continued through to the front of the gas station and parked. He'd go on foot from here. No telling how much Eddie would be able to hear in the canyon if he drove over the road searching for Clar. On foot he'd be able to stay hidden and in the growing shadows.

He stepped from the SUV. He'd never been in a ghost town before and it sure felt like he was in one now. Some of the buildings along the streets were store fronts supported by massive poles, while others were fully constructed with rooms and furniture. Nothing stirred except the sun setting in the west, sinking slowly behind the hills of the canyon.

He walked around the station surveying his surroundings. Jimmy didn't think Eddie would be stupid enough to hold up in the first full building so he didn't bother searching the station. Instead, he followed the road along the west outer parameter and approached a white building with caution. Sneaking in the door, he surveyed the empty shell. Nothing.

Continuing his trek, Jimmy passed a vintage airplane sitting idle waiting for some stunt man to pilot and give him the freedom of flying. Following the curve of the road, he ducked into the shadows of an empty town. One by one he opened doors, peering into windows along the way. Discouragement crept in.

What if they'd been wrong about the movie set? What if Eddie had planted the information, knowing full well they'd run with it?

What if Clar was being held somewhere under their noses at an obvious location? He had to stop thinking about what ifs and find out if Clar was here or not.

Jimmy's phone vibrated in his front pocket, jolting him a few inches. *Fuck, now what?* He slipped the cell out, gazing down at the message.

HAVE SEARCH WARRANT. 20 MILES OUT. WAIT.

Yeah, well, the way he saw it, his goose was already cooked, no way was he waiting. With only one more section of the ranch to check, he saw no reason to quit now. By the time Jacki and Clint arrived he planned for it to be all over. He'd either be dead along with Clar or Eddie would be. Either way, he was going in.

He stepped out from behind the shell of a building, the sky turning the dusty gray of twilight. Wouldn't be long now and daylight would vanish completely. If the sky stayed clear, he'd only have the moon to light his way along the fake small town's main street. He didn't have time to wait for the cops to show up.

He had to move on to check the last few buildings. He saw no other option; time was running out.

"I'll be back after a pee break. Don't go anywhere, sweetheart." Laughter resonated from the diner two buildings away. "Ha, as if you could go somewhere anyway."

A door slammed shut. Jimmy ducked into an open door, froze, and stayed out of sight. His heart racing, a pain shot through his chest snatching his breath away. He gulped down several breaths to steady his nerves. As his body settled its beat, a shadow passed by. He peered around the corner, through the door as the body continued its journey. Long, unruly hair lifted in the breeze. A plain brown prairie style skirt dusted the top of a pair of boots—combat boots.

Looks like Evie. Sounds like Evie. It can't be. She's back in LA. She wouldn't set me up, would she? Is she working with her brother? No, even Evie wouldn't have allowed anyone to tie her up the way they'd found her for the sake of deception. There had been real fear in her eyes. Eddie is here dressed in Evie's clothes. Clar is in that building—alive!

Jimmy watched the figure disappear into another one of the completed buildings on the other side of the street. He edged into the fading light and worked his way silently to the building he hoped Clar was in. It seemed to take an hour to schlep the hundred feet to that doorway. When he looked inside Clar sat in a chair surrounded by an eerie yellow light, her hands bound above her head, and a dark mask over her eyes.

Her normally spiked hair was a flat mess. She licked her lips then cocked her head towards him. His heart thundered in his chest. She was alive.

He quickly scanned the vintage diner, finding no one else in the movie set Jimmy took a step further inside.

"Back so soon, asshole?" she quipped with a fearlessness Jimmy didn't know she had in her.

"Shhhh, Clar, it's Jimmy." He scurried across the room, pulling the mask from Clar's face. He gently cupped her face in his hands, a thumb tracing her parched lips. He wanted to look into her eyes, to know she was really okay. Recognition followed, pushing flood gates open. Tears spilled down over her cheeks. "Are you okay, Clar? Did the son-of-a-bitch hurt you in any way?"

"Jimmy, how—" Clar sucked in the sob, her eyes glistening with moisture, relief, and something he'd never seen directed at him before—love. His lips trailed kisses over her cheeks, capturing each salty tear as it fell.

"There's no time for that. I'm here and we've got to get you to safety." Jimmy worked the knot around her wrists keeping her arms tied to the pillar above her head. His fingers fumbling with the rope, panic struck his mind. "Damn, that fucker knows knots."

Jimmy finally got the knot loose enough to pull on it, only to tighten it once again. "Fuck you, Eddie DeLuca!" He began to rework the knot, careful not to repeat his last mistake.

"Eddie DeLuca?" Clar sobbed, her resolve melting. "That monster is Evie's brother?"

"That's not even the half of it. As soon as I get you out of here, I'll explain everything. Right now, I've got to get you untied before your arms fall off." Jimmy got the knot loose again, pulling the rope through one loop at a time.

"Hurry, Jimmy, he'll be back any second now," Clar cried softly, her gaze focused on the door.

CHAPTER 17

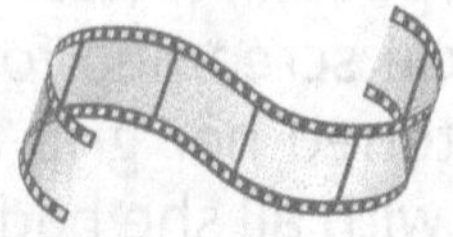

"Well, well, well. What have we here?"

Clar's arms felt weak and limp. Jimmy stood between her and Eddie. She glanced around Jimmy and sucked in a breath. Cradled in Eddie's arms were various items used to enhance sexual pleasure. The more dangerous ones being those used for autoerotic play. These were the type of items found near Dylan at the time of his murder. He'd been filming a simulated breath control segment for the studio. Something Clar had found a bit over the top, even for

Cum Again. She'd had a long, heated argument with Evie about the concept and how keeping up with the latest trend may prove dangerous. Sadly, Clar had been correct.

"Jimmy, he means to hang me." Clar grabbed Jimmy's arm, pulling him closer. An image of the noose swung over a beam with a body dangling from it flashed through her mind. Her mind focused on the face, a face she'd loved for a long time—Jimmy. Blood raced through her with rapid speed, her heart started pounding. Every muscle screamed for her to flee, instead she tightened her grip around Jimmy's arm squeezing with all she had.

His muscles twitched under the pressure. She didn't have to look at Jimmy's face to know he already ran all the possibilities through his mind. She felt his body tense and harden, waiting to make his move on Eddie. Her fingers flexed around his forearm before releasing her hold on him.

"My dear Clar, you are so perceptive. Of course, it'll look like the two of you were getting off with a little self-gratification that went too far," Eddie sang joyously, his expression hidden in the shadows. "And now I'll have double the fun, double the pleasure. Thank you for coming to her rescue, such as it is. I'm looking forward to one of you watching the other get off. Ooh, I'm getting hard just talking about it."

"The fuck you will!" Jimmy lunged forward, but Eddie was quicker and dodged to the right. Jimmy stumbled head first into the closed door, his hands keeping him upright from crashing to the floor.

"You have to be quicker than that my friend. I do so admire your valiant effort though. You are going to be so much fun to play with." Eddie swung the hangman's noose at Jimmy's head, knocking him to the ground.

"Jimmy!" Clar bolted, toppling from the chair, her legs still bound.

Jimmy rolled, but not far enough. Eddie landed on him with a thud, punching and fighting to get the noose around his neck. "Yes, yes, keep struggling newspaper man. I'm so enjoying this. You can feel it, can't you? My excitement rock hard against your stomach."

I've got to get his attention long enough before he beats Jimmy to death. God, please don't let him die like this. Please, I beg you. Clar sucked back the whimper threatening to surface. Any show of fear would only ignite Eddie's sick passion. She had to play on what he initially wanted from her—her father's list. Her arms still weak from lack of blood flow, she forced them down where her fingers clumsily worked the knots of the rope binding her legs.

"Eddie! It's me you want, not him," Clar yelled across the room, the knots looser than they were a few moments ago, but not enough to free herself. "What good will it do you to kill him?"

Eddie stopped wrestling Jimmy, rolled off him, and smirked at Clar. "You may be right. Killing him wouldn't prove anything or help me get what's mine."

Clar winced as Jimmy sputtered and coughed, blood running from his nose. He gasped for air and Clar returned her gaze back to Eddie lurking a few feet from the door.

"That's right, Eddie. You want the list, remember. The list my dad had." Clar continued to wiggle her ankles, hoping the motion would work to loosen the ropes a bit more. If she could get up, she might be able to make a run for it. Eddie would chase her and it might give Jimmy enough time to escape or call for help.

"Ah yes, I almost forgot. The list that will give me power and leadership in the family." Eddie's eyes twinkled with excitement, his body looming above her.

"Tell me, Eddie. Before you take your pleasure with me, tell me how to please so that I know when I've given you all that you want." Clar licked her lips, doing her best to bring Kandi out of hiding. If being sexual was what he wanted, then she'd give it to him the only way she knew how—by acting the part.

Something in Eddie's face changed. It became crazed, sex crazed. She'd seen that look on men before when she'd done promo events. With any luck, she had him right where she wanted him. Thirsting for her to distraction.

"My dear Kandi, you've given me an abundance of pleasure through the years." Eddie knelt down beside her, his fingers a whisper across her cheek. "If there was any other way to get the list other than killing you, believe me, I would. I'd take you back home and make you my personal sex toy."

"Why can't you still do that, Eddie?" Clar purred, leaning into his touch. "You could have it all. The list. The family business. And exclusive access to me, twenty-four seven."

"Believe me, it's a tempting concept." Eddie continued to stroke her hair, the short strands sliding through his fingertips. "Big problem though."

"A problem too big for a man like you to handle?" Clar coaxed, snuggling against his knee.

"Maybe not a problem, really. Just an obstacle that needs to be removed." Eddie's hand floated over her breast, sending shivers of disgust through her.

"There is no obstacle too big that Eddie DeLuca can't handle. That's what I've always heard." Clar complimented in hopes of playing on his vanity.

"Hmm, I'm not sure how you'd feel giving yourself to me after all that has happened. Hell, I know I don't want to share the family wealth with my sister. And I certainly wouldn't want to share you with the SOB laying across the room." Eddie smiled, kissing her forehead with a tender kiss. "But I think big sister needs to die in order for me to have everything. She's the entire puzzle while you, Dylan, Levi, Cameron, and even Father have merely been the pieces."

A shadow rose from near the door, and Clar sucked in a breath. Her gaze quickly returned to Eddie, raking over his face. He hadn't noticed Jimmy struggling to reach the door.

Lifting his head Jimmy moaned, an eye felt swollen and a hint of blood lingered in the corner of his mouth. Somewhere in the dull yellow light, he heard Clar talking as Eddie knelt over her. What were they talking about? Was DeLuca starting his dirty work on Clar? Jimmy's vision began to clear a bit as his mind swam through the faint swirling in his head.

He had to get the world to stop spinning. He had to get up and over to Clar. Focusing again on her, his vision began to clear.

Somehow Clar had gotten to the floor, her legs trapped against the chair. *If that son of a bitch hurts her in any way, I'll kill him if it takes my last dying breath.*

Rolling onto his side, Jimmy groped for anything that would give him leverage to get on his feet. His fingers grabbed the edge of a toppled table and he struggled to pull himself upright. A pain shot through his ribs knocking him back to his knees. He sucked in a breath and pulled his body up again. Everything around him spinning slightly, he barely made out the floor beneath his feet.

"There's no obstacle..." Clar's voice cooed through the fog in Jimmy's head. What the hell was she trying to do, seduce the asshole? Surely not, unless she felt there was no other way. Clar had to be stalling to give him time to maneuver.

Jimmy gradually shuffled toward them, catching Clar's attention for a brief moment. She hastily smiled than leaned into Eddie. "You are a master, Mr. DeLuca. So talented at deception, it's incredible how you managed to trick us all. This kind of talent must run in your family for you to be so amazingly clever."

"I think the best was at the hospital." Eddie's voice emulated pride, his body stance upright with confidence. "Or maybe it was in your place when I bought some candy. They all were so much fun and scripted to a tee."

"The hospital?" Clar's gaze met Jimmy's as he moved in closer.

"Yes, the day you and your friends were visiting Levi. Remember that little old lady you helped as she leaned into the wall on her cane?" Eddie straightened his spine like a peacock showing off his tail feathers. "I almost laughed out loud. Even in my mind I'd hoped you may have thought it was Evie, making things easier for me to get rid of her. After all, I imagine how she must despise you and your sexual flare with the men. Your beauty outshines her plainness ten-fold even with changes in your appearance. You are an exceptionally sexy full-figured woman."

"That was you?" Clar looked at Jimmy over Eddie's shoulder. Jimmy nodded then rushed forward, tripping over the forgotten noose, and landed on Eddie's back.

"You asshole!" Jimmy hissed, rolling the two of them away from Clar. "You'll not be so lucky this time to have a weapon at your disposal."

Eddie bucked then scampered out from under Jimmy. He scurried to his feet, stumbling behind the counter.

"Come out from behind there," Jimmy ordered, helping Clar to her feet. "You've got nowhere to hide any more. We've seen everything. All the pictures. Your plans to kill Clar and then Evie. Maybe even Cameron is on your death list."

"You are so wrong. You don't understand who I am. What power I have," Eddie spat, his crazed gaze darted around the room.

Jimmy watched Eddie sway back and forth behind the counter like a lion in the zoo waiting for dinner. The man was losing it quickly now that his plans had been disrupted.

"Clar, are you okay?" Jimmy glanced over his shoulder. He wanted to hear her voice, making sure she was fine.

"Yes," Clar said, her voice strong and clear. "He didn't hurt me."

Jimmy turned his attention back to Eddie, seemingly trapped behind the counter. The only way he'd be able to reach the door was if he jumped over the counter and made a run for it. Jimmy wasn't sure if Eddie actually had the brains, or the strength after their tussle, to make it that far. Hell, Jimmy wasn't sure he had the ability to get to him before the jerk made it out the door.

"What is so important that you had to kill for it? A piece of paper saying you would own property? Is it worth going to prison for?" Jimmy taunted, looking for an opportunity to lunge across the counter.

In the yellowed light Eddie continued to pace nervously behind the bar like a caged animal. "Power. All that property. All the bank accounts. And that fucking list Turner had. They will give me power to run the DeLuca empire as I see fit. Not the way my father has run it into the ground. But to bring it back to its glory days. Then I'll have California once Evie..." Eddie stopped abruptly; his mouth snapping shut. Jimmy followed Eddie's startled look to the shadow figure standing just outside the door.

"Are you referring to the list of officials on daddy's payroll locked up in my safe?" Evie stood in the doorway, walking slowly toward her twin, her hands raised in surrender. "The old ways are gone, Eddie."

"Evie, when..." Jimmy swung his arm out, keeping Clar from stepping out from behind him. If this was going to be a showdown of the twins, he didn't want Clar in the line of fire.

"What's Evie doing here? How did she get daddy's list?" Clar asked.

"I don't know, Clar. I thought I was the only one to have it." Jimmy took a step forward then halted when he caught the look on Evie's face. If she could keep Eddie busy, he might be able to get in behind him and take him out of commission.

"You have that list?" Clar stiffened, moving away from him.

"It's sealed and in a safety deposit box." Jimmy reached for Clar, his heart sinking when she pushed his hand away. "Obviously, I'm not the only one with a copy."

Evie shook her head, focused on Eddie. "This is why daddy split up the family properties, Eddie. He knew I loved being in California. He also believed you loved living in Chicago, where you have always belonged." Evie smiled sweetly, her eyes lighting up with love. She cared about her brother despite all that he'd done to her. Despite the deaths he had been responsible for. Despite everything, he was her brother.

Eddie's focus shifted to Evie. "I thought I'd take care of you later today, but you've saved me the trip, sister dear. And since I know you have Turner's list, I'll have no use for any of you."

"Eddie, do you think mother would have liked to see us this way? Fighting over the very thing that kept her from the love of her life?" Evie kept moving closer, stepping over the sex paraphernalia scattered on the floor. "The life of a mobster's lover is a hard one. Momma lost her entire family because of that love. Her bitterness towards her family soured me as well for years."

Jimmy edged toward the wall behind the bar. Inch by inch he crept his way closer.

"Mother would be proud to see I'd taken over the business, Evie." Eddie leaned into the counter, his body losing some of its tension.

"No, no she wouldn't. Not like this." Evie stood a few feet from her brother, her body relaxed, posing no threat whatsoever. "She would have wanted us to embrace our family. That's why her brother kept copies of the list. She wouldn't have wanted to see us hurt the people she loved deep in her heart."

"Yes, she would have!" Eddie yelled, his fists banging against the countertop. "She would have been happy to see Sal die at the hands—humph."

Jimmy had leapt, his arms wrapping around Eddie's shoulders, pulling him to the ground. Bottles crashed to the floor as Eddie thrashed out with his arms. Jimmy held on, pinning Eddie's back against the floor, holding his arms down. Evie jumped over the counter, pulled her brother from Jimmy's grasp and into her arms, rocking him softly.

"It's all over now, little brother." Evie said, soothing her whimpering brother. "You're safe. No one will hurt you again."

"Police! Come out and no one will get hurt!"

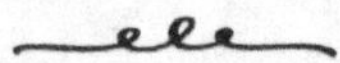

A spotlight flashed across the room. Clar put a hand up to shield her eyes from the blinding brightness. "It's Clar Turner. Everyone is okay. Can you please put down that light, you're blinding me." She glared at Cameron, her heart working its way out of her stomach.

"Would someone mind telling me what the hell is going on here?" Cameron demanded, gun drawn, waving the light around the disheveled room until it reached Jimmy with his arms around Clar.

Clar kneeled on the floor next to Evie. "The road will be rough, and long, but worth it," she promised Evie, stroking her back in small circles like a mother soothing her troubled child. "I won't leave you until it's all over."

"It's a long bazaar story about family, lust, power, and money," Clar said to Cameron, watching Evie rock Eddie in her arms. "I'm not sure you'd fully understand, or even believe it."

"Well, hell. Why not give me a try then so I can put this SOB in prison for life." Cameron walked across the threshold into the building. Jacki and Clint close behind, revolvers in their hands. "Eddie DeLuca's got to pay for what he did to Dylan. What he'd planned to do to you and Evie, not to mention the assault on Levi and the murders."

"Go easy on Clar, Cameron, she's had one hell of a night here," Jimmy strongly suggested, pulling Clar back into his arms. "You'll get the facts, but first let's get everyone out of this hell hole."

The strength and security of his arm around her had Clar thinking of *forever*. This man would have done anything to find her when he could have left it to the law. Instead, he'd put himself in danger. If that wasn't a form of love then Clar didn't know what was. She wished she'd realized it before it had become a life-or-death situation to open her eyes, and heart, to Jimmy's love.

The distant wail of sirens echoed through the canyon. The cavalry was arriving. It would only be a matter of minutes before they'd rip Eddie from Evie's arms. Even now, after everything that had happened over the past several hours, Clar wasn't sure she'd be able to watch that materialize. There was obviously a bond between the twins that even the mob couldn't break, and she wasn't so sure that's what Sal DeLuca had intended anyway. Once they got back to the precinct, opened those sealed documents belonging to her dad, they might have a better understanding of the connection between Evie, Eddie, and herself.

She could speculate why her dad chose Jimmy and Evie to receive copies of a list she knew nothing about. Hell, they would all be speculating now as Eddie DeLuca was cuffed and put into the back of a squad. Evie Dagmyer, quiet as a mouse, climbed into Clint's truck with Jacki. Cameron jumped into his vehicle and led the pack back to LA, unaware of the full extent of events that had taken place.

Jimmy's arms went around Clar's waist, pulling her against him. Her feet left the ground and she snuggled into the cradle of his shoulder. "James O'Brien, don't you ever let me go again, you hear me?"

Jimmy welcomed her lips and his heat rushed through her. "Not on my plan for the future, Clarice Turner."

CHAPTER 18

Clar pulled the SUV up to the store front. She'd finally closed on her house and packed the last of her home and business into boxes several days ago, while Jimmy moved his belongings from California weeks ahead of her. In a few hours the moving van would arrive from Wisconsin to Black Horse Canyon in Oklahoma. Her once new life would return to her with a freshness she'd not imagined a few months ago.

After all the pain and suffering, Edward Dagmyer DeLuca was isolated behind bars awaiting evaluation and only semi aware of what he'd done. Clar held a sadness in her heart. A well-kept family secret, her father, Karl Turner, for years had made valiant attempts to convince his sister, Isabel Turner Anderson, to bring her twin babies home to live with them. He'd promised to care for her and the babies until she could afford to live on her own. But Belle wouldn't leave Salvador DeLuca, not even for her own family. She loved Sal, truly loved him despite him being a mobster. Clar believed Sal loved her Aunt Belle just as much. An aunt Clar herself never knew existed.

Sal had done the only thing he could without uprooting his own family at home, make sure Belle and their twins, Evie and Eddie, were well taken care of. He'd managed to convince his wife to allow him to bring home the little boy in need of his daddy.

Karl Turner found a way to make sure DeLuca honored his promise to Belle. He kept a list of every person in Chicago who'd ever done a "favor" for Sal. Held it as insurance that his sister, and niece and nephew, would continue under Sal's protection.

As Eddie grew from a loving little boy to a bitter young man, he wanted everything Sal had. He'd found out about the list that would expose Sal. He hired a rogue hit man to have Clar's parents killed, and then a few years later planned to have Dylan Cameron murdered at the studio once Evie took it over.

His planning progressed when Eddie realized his plain looking sister had pangs of jealousy towards Clar. Eddie admitted in court to being equally jealous of her himself, but for different reasons. While Evie appeared jealous of Clar's movie star looks, Eddie envied her sex appeal and harbored aspirations to be like her.

As Sal's health began to fade, Eddie perceived Dylan Cameron's death as a way to keep his sister, and Cameron, at bay. Eddie wanted the DeLuca family empire to himself. He'd thought by killing Clar, Evie would be blamed and her apparent suicide as a sign of guilt.

Levi had been a pawn in the scheme of things. After Clar quit the business, Eddie used Levi to draw her back to LA. He'd make her death look like Evie did it out of jealousy. It had almost worked.

Now with Eddie behind bars with a life sentence looming, Evie was his only visitor. Cameron had returned to Chicago, retired as a detective, and became a private investigator helping families locate missing loved ones.

"Clar?" Jimmy's voice drew her from the memories of those awful times.

"Hey." Clar smiled, looking at him. "What's up?"

"You alright?" Jimmy asked, putting the final touches on the window of Clar's new candy store.

"Yeah, just thinking about Evie and how much we missed because we hadn't grown up together as cousins." Clar strolled over and wiped a splatter of pink paint from his face. "Thank you for coming out ahead of me and getting things ready. But I think you might be getting more on you than the window."

Clar looked away at the sound of horse's hooves. Jacki came riding up the street on Max, her black stallion. Halting in front of the store, Jacki slid out of the saddle, then tied Max to the hitching post. Her best friend had returned to her ranch life with a former Texas Ranger hot on her heels.

"Now that's something I'll have to get used to, you riding into town on Max." Clar walked over, stroking the horse's glistening black neck. "Don't worry, big guy, I'm making some special candy kisses just for you."

"You're going to spoil the heck out of him." Jacki placed the ring of keys in her hand, giving it a squeeze. "Here's an extra set of keys for the shop. There's an apartment upstairs that's yours as well. I had it cleaned up for you, but you may want to put your own little touches on it. The place is yours for as long as you want to stay."

"Only if I can provide you and Max with all the treats you can devour." Clar said, her fingers closing around the ring.

"Looks like you've come home, Clar." Jimmy's voice teased her ear and a shiver of heat raced through her. His arms wrapped around Clar from behind, and she sighed.

Clar leaned her head against his shoulder, then turned, folding her hands around his neck. "I'm never leaving again without you, Jimmy." She rose on her boot covered toes, kissing him fully on the mouth. Clar pulled away, watching the moving van drive up their dusty road.

"Yes, we're finally home."

CHECK OUT MORE GREAT READS FROM ROWAN PROSE!

Maxine Douglas writes in several genres, including historical romance and romantic suspense. She is a current member of the Oklahoma Writers' Federation, Inc. and its affiliations, Central Region Oklahoma Writers, and Oklahoma Romance Writers Guild. A widow and Wisconsin native, Maxine now resides in Oklahoma.